THE ICE AT THE
BOTTOM OF THE WORLD

STORIES BY

MARK RICHARD

ALFRED A. KNOPF   NEW YORK   1989

THE ICE AT
THE BOTTOM OF
THE WORLD

THIS IS A BORZOI BOOK

PUBLISHED BY ALFRED A. KNOPF, INC.

The author expresses his thanks to those publications in which his work was originally published: *Antaeus, Equator, Esquire, The Quarterly,* and *Shenandoah.* Some of these stories have also been published in the anthologies *From Mt. San Angelo, New Stories from the South,* and *Pushcart Prize.*

Library of Congress Cataloging-in-Publication Data

Richard, Mark, [date]
    The ice at the bottom of the world / Mark Richard.
        p. cm.
    ISBN 0-394-56485-5
    I. Title.
PS3568.I313I24   1989   813'.54—dc19   88-25947

Manufactured in the United States of America
First Edition

TO CLAIRE

CONTENTS

Thank you, God, for all my friends always having for me a pillow and a blanket, a place at the table, some dollars to put in my pocket. Bless especially the boys from the original Thunderbird Lounge—Brian, Scott, Melvin, Terry, John, Joe, Carl, and Stan. Bless the Eminent Cheese and Hola, Casey and Denise. Bless Gordon; Tom, too. Rest Jim Boatwright. Bless the girls Maggie and Temperance and Julie, and bless that one girl, Pamela Sue, whose faith never fails and whose love always brightens. Bless them all and thanks again.

Yrs., M.R.

THE ICE AT THE
BOTTOM OF THE WORLD

STRAYS

AT NIGHT, stray dogs come up underneath our house to lick our leaking pipes. Beneath my brother and my's room we hear them coughing and growling, scratching their ratted backs against the boards beneath our beds. We lie awake, listening, my brother thinking of names to name the one he is setting out to catch. Salute and Topboy are high on his list.

I tell my brother these dogs are wild and cowering. A bare-heeled stomp on the floor off our beds sends them scuttling spine-bowed out the crawl-space beneath our open window. Sometimes, when my brother is quick, he leans out and touches one slipping away.

Our father has meant to put the screens back on the

windows for spring. He has even hauled them out of the storage shed and stacked them in the drive. He lays them one by one over sawhorses to tack in the frames tighter and weave patches against mosquitoes. This is what he means to do, but our mother that morning pulls all the preserves off the shelves onto the floor, sticks my brother and my's Easter Sunday drawings in her mouth, and leaves the house through the field next door cleared the week before for corn.

Uncle Trash is our nearest relative with a car and our mother has a good half-day head start on our father when Uncle Trash arrives. Uncle Trash runs his car up the drive in a big speed, splitting all the screens stacked there from their frames. There is an exploded chicken in the grill of Uncle Trash's car. They don't even turn the motor off as Uncle Trash slides out and our father gets behind the wheel, backing back over the screens, setting out in search of our mother.

Uncle Trash finds out that he has left his bottle under the seat of his car. He goes into our kitchen, pulling out all the shelves our mother missed. Then he is in the towel box in the hall, looking, pulling out stuff in stacks. He is in our parents' room, opening short doors. He is in the storage shed, opening and sniffing a mason jar of gasoline for the power mower. Uncle Trash comes up and asks, Which way it is to town for a drink. I point up the road. Uncle Trash sets off, saying, Don't y'all burn the house down.

4

My brother and I hang out in the side yard, doing handstands until dark. We catch handfuls of lightning bugs and smear bright yellow on our shirts. It is late. I wash our feet and put us to bed. We wait for somebody to come back home but nobody ever does. Lucky for me when my brother begins to whine for our mother the stray dogs show up under the house. My brother starts making up lists of new names for them, naming himself to sleep.

Hungry, we wake up to something sounding in the kitchen not like our mother fixing us anything to eat.

It is Uncle Trash. He is throwing up and spitting blood into the pump-handled sink. I ask him did he have an accident and he sends my brother upstairs for merthiolate and Q-tips. His face is angled out from his head on one side so that-sided eye is shut. His good eye waters when he wiggles loose teeth with cut-up fingers.

Uncle Trash says he had an accident, all right. He says he was up in a card game and then he was real up in a card game, so up he bet his car, accidentally forgetting that our father had driven off with it in search of our mother. Uncle Trash says the man who won the card game went ahead and beat up Uncle Trash on purpose anyway.

All day Uncle Trash sleeps in our parents' room. We in the front yard can hear him snoring. My brother and

I dig in the dirt with spoons, making roadbeds and high-
ways for my tin metal trucks. In the evening, Uncle
Trash comes down in one of our father's shirts, dirty,
but cleaner than the one he had gotten beat up in. We
have banana sandwiches for supper. Uncle Trash asks
do we have a deck of cards in the house. He says he
wants to see do his tooth-cut fingers still bend enough
to work. I have to tell him how our mother disallows
card-playing in the house but that my brother has a pack
of Old Maid somewhere in the toy box. While my
brother goes out to look I brag at how I always beat my
brother out, leaving him the Old Maid, and Uncle Trash
says, Oh, yeah? and digs around in his pocket for a
nickel he puts on the table. He says, We'll play a nickel
a game. I go into my brother and my's room to get the
Band-Aid box of nickels and dimes I sometimes short
from the collection plate on Sunday.

Uncle Trash is making painful faces, flexing his red-
painted fingers around the Old Maid deck of circus-star
cards, but he still shuffles, cuts, and deals a three-way
hand one-handed—and not much longer, I lose my
Band-Aid box of money and all the tin metal trucks of
mine out in the front yard. Uncle Trash makes me go
out and get them and put them on his side of the table.
My brother loses a set of bowling pins and a stuffed
beagle. In two more hands, we stack up our winter boots
and coats with the hoods on Uncle Trash's side of the
table. In the last hand, my brother and I step out of our

6

shorts and underdrawers while Uncle Trash smiles, saying, And now, gentlemen, if you please, the shirts off y'all's backs.

Uncle Trash rakes everything my brother and I owned into the pillowcases off our bed and says let that be a lesson to me. He is off through the front porch door, leaving us buck-naked at the table, his last words as he goes up the road, shoulder-slinging his loot, Don't y'all burn the house down.

I am burning hot at Uncle Trash.

Then I am burning hot at our father for leaving us with him to look for our mother.

Then I am burning hot at my mother for running off, leaving me with my brother, who is rubber-chinning and face-pouting his way into a good cry.

There is only one thing left to do, and that is to take all we still have left that we own and throw it at my brother—and I do—and Old Maid cards explode on his face, setting him off on a really good howl.

I tell my brother that making so much noise will keep the stray dogs away, and he believes it, and then I start to believe it when it gets later than usual, past the crickets and into a long moon over the trees, but they finally do come after my brother finally does fall asleep, so I just wait until I know there are several strays beneath the bed boards, scratching their rat-matted backs and growling, and I stomp on the floor, what is my favorite part about the dogs, stomping and then watching them

scatter in a hundred directions and then seeing them
one by one collect in a pack at the edge of the field near
the trees.

In the morning right off I recognize the bicycle coming wobble-wheeling into the front yard. It's the one the
colored boy outside Cuts uses to run lunches and ice
water to the pulpwood truck Mr. Cuts has working cut-
over timber on the edge of town. The colored boy that
usually drives the bicycle snaps bottlecaps off his fingers
at my brother and I when we go to Cuts with our mother
to make groceries. We have to wait outside by the ker-
osene pump, out by the tar-papered lean-to shed, the
pop-crate place where the men sit around and Uncle
Trash does his card work now. White people generally
don't go into Cuts unless they have to buy on credit.

We at school know Mr. and Mrs. Cuts come from a
family that eats children. There is a red metal tree with
plastic-wrapped toys in the window and a long candy
counter case inside to lure you in. Mr. and Mrs. Cuts
have no children of their own. They ate them during a
hard winter and salted the rest down for sandwiches
the colored boy runs out to the pulpwood crew at noon.
I count colored children going in to buy some candy to
see how many make it back out, but generally our
mother is ready to go home way before I can tell. Our
credit at Cuts is short.

The front tire catches in one of our tin metal truck's underground tunnels and Uncle Trash takes a spill. The cut crate bolted to the bicycle handlebars spills brown paper packages sealed with electrical tape out into the yard along with a case of Champale and a box of cigars. Uncle Trash is down where he falls. He lays asleep all day under the tree in the front yard, moving only just to crawl back into the wandering shade.

We have for supper sirloins, Champale, and cigars. Uncle Trash teaches how to cross our legs up on the table after dinner, but says he'll go ahead and leave my brother and my's cigars unlit. There is no outlook for our toys and my Band-Aid can of nickels and dimes, checking all the packages, even checking twice again the cut crate bolted on the front of the bicycle. Uncle Trash shows us a headstand on the table while drinking a bottle of Champale, then he stands in the sink and sings "Gather My Farflung Thoughts Together." My brother and I chomp our cigars and clap but in our hearts we are low and lonesome.

Don't y'all burn down the house, says Uncle Trash, pedaling out the yard to Cuts.

My brother leans out our window with a rope coil and sirloin scraps strung on strings. He is in a greasy-fingered sleep when the strings slither like white snakes off our bed, over the sill, out into the fields beyond.

. . . . . .

9

There's July corn and no word from our parents.

Uncle Trash doesn't remember the Fourth of July or the Fourth of July parade. Uncle Trash bunches cattails in the fenders of his bicycle and clips our Old Maid cards in the spokes and follows the fire engine through town with my brother and I in the front cut-out crate throwing penny candy to the crowds. What are you trying to be? the colored men at Cuts ask Uncle Trash when we end up the parade there. I spot a broken-wheeled tin metal truck of mine in a colored child's hand, driving it in circles by the Cuts front steps. Foolish, says Uncle Trash.

Uncle Trash doesn't remember winning Mrs. Cuts in a card game for a day to come out and clean the house and us in the bargain. She pushes the furniture around with a broom and calls us abominations. There's a bucket of soap to wash our heads and a jar of sour-smelling cream for our infected bites, fleas from under the house, and mosquitoes through the windows. The screens are rusty squares in the driveway dirt. Uncle Trash leaves her his razor opened as long as my arm. She comes after my brother and I with it to cut our hair, she says. We know better. My brother dives under the house and I am up a tree.

Uncle Trash doesn't remember July, but when we tell him about it, he says it sounds like July was probably a good idea at the time.

·　·　·　·　·　·

It is August with the brown, twisted corn in the fields next to the house. There is word from our parents. They are in the state capital. One of them has been in jail. Uncle Trash is still promising screens. We get from Cuts bug spray instead.

I wake up in the middle of a night. My brother floats through the window. Out in the yard, he and a stray have each other on the end of a rope. He reels her in and I make the tackle. Already I feel the fleas leave her rag-matted coat and crawl over my arms and up my neck. We spray her down with a whole can of bug spray until her coat lathers like soap. My brother gets some matches to burn a tick like a grape out of her ear. The touch of the match covers her like a blue-flame sweater. She's a fireball shooting beneath the house.

By the time Uncle Trash and the rest of town get there, the Fire Warden says the house is Fully Involved.

In the morning I see our parents drive past where our house used to be. I see them go by again until they recognize the yard. Uncle Trash is trying to bring my brother out of the trance he is in by showing him how some tricks work on the left-standing steps of the stoop. Uncle Trash shows Jack-Away, Queen in the Whorehouse, and No Money Down. Our father says for Uncle Trash to stand up so he can knock him down. Uncle Trash says he deserves that one. Our father knocks Uncle Trash down again and tells him not to get up. If

11

you get up I'll kill you, our father says.

Uncle Trash crawls on all fours across our yard out to the road.

Goodbye, Uncle Trash, I say.

Goodbye, men! Uncle Trash says. Don't y'all burn the house down! he says, and I say, We won't.

During the knocking-down nobody notices our mother. She is a flat-footed running rustle through the corn all burned up by the summer sun.

HER FAVORITE STORY

In Indian, this place is called Where Lightning Takes Tall Walks. I figure that to be about right. What happens here is this is the first landfall those water-heavy thunderheads make when they quick-boil up from across the bay. Long-legged stretches of bone-white light come kicking through the treetops of the tallest shortleaf pines, ripping limbs and splitting crowns. When they leave past, your ears are ringing from the thundershots and there is the smell about of electric-seared sap. It is a heart-racer to have happen around you in the day, and at night you still have coming to you the cracking hiss and branching swish in the whole dark of crowns falling so heavy unseen and so close

13

they push air past your face and the ground bounces you up on your toes.

What I am out here doing in this place where lightning takes tall walks has to do with what happened with me and Margaret when we lived a cable length upriver. My cabin is actually three bends and a cutback along the shore from here and I imagine by now it is run over with raccoons and field mice and black snakes coming in for to eat them. I don't imagine anybody has run off with anything in it, seeing how the rut down to where my cabin is is generally under a flood tide and mostly washed out up along the last three miles it runs out to the county road. I swam by one day recently and it seems to be all right, allowing for the tree trunk stuck in the roof and excepting for one of the all-glass front windows that is busted out, probably shot that way from somebody in a boat. The big-headed dog I brought home for Margaret wasn't around, me reckoning now he has run off back to town.

Town is where he came from that I got him, from one of those big turnaround truck drivers who used a softball bat on the animal, saying the dog was mean. The big-headed dog wasn't mean, though he was wall-eyed, and wall-eyed isn't something you want to see on a dog—meaning they're not too bright, not good for tracking or running a trace. That turnaround truck driver got drunk in town—it was a Friday—and beat that big-headed dog with the softball bat until he bled from his ears and tail and then threw the dog off the end of Rusty Shackleford's dock. Lucky for the dog it was near low tide so he could lay passed out in half a hand of water without drowning. I had no carry with the turnaround driver with the softball bat, but the dog wasn't dead at all and it was to have a hard death in the water, cold from a four-day freeze, so I laid the old beat-up mutt on a pound net I had in the bottom of my metal flake canoe and paddled us on home.

Home, I pulled open down the oven door, laying the dog on it under broil to warm him up and dry him out, and what but if the first thing he didn't do, coming around awake, was to try to take off my damn arm at the shoulder, chasing me around my own house, me finally up on the picnic table I had in my living room and him yapping and snappy, barking below with steam coming off his coat from the oven broil like he was some sort of demon dog from hell.

What it was I never knew Margaret had that settled that big-headed dog, wild as he was, him snockering around her like a puppy, not letting me raise my voice at her lest I get a growl from where he used to sleep most of the time by the alpine hearth. It was just the way she was, the way she had with people, men and dogs alike. She wasn't beautiful and it didn't matter, them even in town not saying she was beautiful, though I could tell, by the way Rusty Shackleford and Danny Daniels Shackleford and Scoop looked down her shirt sideways under her arms, seeing she had an all-over tan at least up top, I could tell that drove them in town wild. What I call town when I say town really being just Rusty Shackleford's seafood house at the end of a half-fell-down dock with two pumps, a diesel and a gas. Town being where Rusty had a hoist for packing out the local high-rise rigs, a concrete-crate shed, and a motel machine for ice, him having between where it is safe to get good last footing before falling through the rotten planks and the crushed-shell turnaround, a desk he calls his office, a one-room five-sided store, and a shoebox near where the cat named Fishhead sleeps in the window, a place where if ever you were to get any mail in this world you would find it there, most likely already opened up and read out loud to everybody by Rusty, drinking on Friday nights in what this place is I call town.

It is in town where, before Margaret, I could get my fill of human life, coming in with a fair wind and following the tide down river, paddling my metal flake canoe to get grub in the five-sided store and take on any nets needing mends.

Rusty's half-cousin Earl Shackleford Hayes being my best customer, seeing how he's always ripping up all his rigs running spot and trout off Stumpy Point, everybody knowing how poor the bottom is there, Rusty saying to him, Why do you think they call it *Stumpy* Point? and then saying to us, Earl's but *half*-cousin, half, half, only just a *half*. Winters, after making groceries and gathering net for work, I'd help in the concrete-crate shed packing boxes of fish, and summers I'd shovel ice, always on Fridays stopping at dark for a drink. Danny Daniels and Scoop would liquor up enough to beat hell out of each other in the crushed-shell turnaround if there weren't any truck drivers to fight with, me putting in with them together when there were. I could make a day and a night of going into this place I call town doing the business and then the get-together fight waiting for the first after-dark tide to turn. So this was town when I say I sometimes later brought Margaret, not so beautiful but driving the rough men wild with her all-over tan, them helping her out of the canoe when we came gliding up like she was an Indian princess, leaving me to tote and carry three loads of mended pound net to the five-sided store all by myself, her having the way she had on the rough men at the dock in town.

The way she had on me, Rusty Shackleford said, was a clean shirt and a combed head. I figure that to be about right, that being what of me he could see away from my cut-off-from-the-world cabin. Cut off from so far away from the world I used to walk the clay-bank shoreline naked with a smear of good mud pulled across my shoulders and over my privates against the sun, an osprey feather tucked behind my ear for chiggers and ticks, that being how me and Margaret first met, her digging relics for the state, her figuring where I lived

17

to be where Indians kept a summer camp long ago, her having to walk about forty lengths of bad shoreline at low tide to get to where she could fill plastic bags and pockets full of the pottery pieces and pipe stems I already have so many of I just step on to break. She said her particular interest in Indians took her aback when she looked up and saw me mud-naked and feather-headed forty lengths from a highway and me being without a girlfriend since a season six or eight back, what I can say is that my particular interest in her showed itself with a growth, breaking little mud flakes crumbling to my toes, one of the ways Margaret always had on me when I looked at her.

What else that Rusty Shackleford didn't know about her having a way on me was how, after I started getting her to stay over from where she dug relics for the state, she started to clean the outdoor things from the front room of my cabin. First out to go were a stack of busted crab pots, some sawhorses holding up the keel of a skiff I'd been thinking about building for three years, four barrels of scrap and trash, a load of termite wood to burn in the alpine hearth, and half a load of washed-up two-by-fours for a someday front porch. She even got me to put all my power saws and axes in the shed, her not knowing how I love to saw and cut up things indoors. What was left was the picnic table to dance on when we drank and listened to Latin records, also my favorite old stuffed chair, and my upright rigs so

18

I could string and mend net throughout the house, her putting screens back up on the windows so flying-through-the-house birds wouldn't foul in the strung-up netting and cripple themselves. We even cleaned out the old alpine hearth so on those afternoons when the flood tide was up in the windward yard and it was raining hammers and nails and a hundred dozen seagulls were softballed in the leeward lawn, we could stretch out on a quilt in front of a fire and drink hot wine and play Monopoly naked with the big-headed dog snoring nearby. This is what Rusty Shackleford could not have been knowing about, how in this cut-off-from-the-world home Margaret was making my life even more than a clean shirt and combed head can say.

In the summer, the secret of her all-over tan was us paddling halfway over the Stingray Point in my metal flake canoe, me putting out the little Danforth anchor I'd found in back of Rusty Shackleford's concrete-crate shed, us naked drinking cold beer laying in the bottom of the canoe, legs crossed over legs and over the side, me telling her the Indian stories I knew, like where lightning takes tall walks and how Stingray Point got its name. That one being her favorite story I used to tell again and again, about Captain John Smith up from Jamestown stinging himself on a stingray, a good story about him spearing fish with his sword and getting stung, his arm swole up and his tongue stuck out, about how they thought he would die so they went ashore out of their boats and dug the grave but instead Smith got drunk off the surgeon's rum and ate the stingray and lived, and they all sailed away, leaving a big empty hole in the ground for the Indians to come out from the woods to look down into, trying to figure out what for and probably not being able to. This stingray story being Margaret's favorite, I used to tell her over and over, her listening, soft-sucking on a beer bottle and playing with my privates with her big, all-over-tanned, naked toe.

In the winter, I used to have to take a butane torch out back to the well house to defreeze the water pump, being careful not to heat up the rocks in the floor to wake the snakes hibernating underneath, this even after, in the sleet and fog somewhere between the cabin and the well house, stumbling through a flock of snow geese on their way south resting in my leeward lawn, their necks as big as your arm, wing muscles strong and hard from their Canada-to-Cuba flight, so big and strong to knock you down if you were to stumble through them, flushing them up unawares which I usually was, so early in the morning fog going out to defreeze the pump.

In that winter Margaret stayed over, she showed how if you patched a light bulb to the electric pump to burn, it would keep the air from freezing while leaving the snakes alone, and then she took Christmas gift pictures of the snow geese eating the corn she had laid out for them, and in the morning with coffee she'd cook up fried eggs and ham from Rusty Shackleford's five-sided store instead of just the candy bar or peanut-butter sandwich I was used to, and this after taking a hot shower together with plenty of hot water pumping up from the well house, me soaping Margaret's back, wondering why hadn't I thought of the light bulb trick before.

That coming spring, a mama raccoon had babies in the woodpile, so getting a fire meant dealing with her trying to tear you up, not even being afraid of the big-headed dog Margaret had fed to full grown by then. Getting a piece or two of wood to burn in the alpine hearth was like playing a big set of pick-up sticks, not wanting to move or bother the whole pile lest the mama coon'd come tearing out hissing and chasing me and the big-headed dog back inside the house. This was something Margaret liked to watch, sometimes taking pictures and sometimes pretending to lock us out with the pissed-off mama coon coming at us on our heels. I stopped getting anything altogether off the pile, settling on burning driftwood, which was a ache and a pain to gather. But the sand in it burned the flames in the fire green and were pretty for us to look at, stretched out naked on the quilt late at night. It came spring soon anyway and we didn't need the fires, and mama coon and what we called the coonettes started coming up on the steps to look in the house and the way Margaret had with people pretty soon the coonettes were all over

21

the place eating out of the dog's bowl and then chasing his tail around the picnic table I still had in the living room for furniture. I only put my foot down the time they all ate the lime rinds we'd had left over from a batch of gin and tonics, and raving and hissing drunk they ripped open my favorite big covered chair and tore out all the stuffing. I think chasing them all out of the house with a broom and a stick hurt Margaret's feelings, and looking back on it now, I feel sorry for doing it.

That is the spring I'm come to tell about, the spring of remembering the mama coon and her babies, what I last remember. And this, the night we were hearing one of those quick-boiling thunderstorms step and kick around the place where lightning takes tall walks, us in the bed in the back bedroom with the big-headed dog sitting on the straight-backed chair to watch like he liked to do, us saying the little secret things to each other that people doing what we were doing say, then me feeling the hair on my arm bend the wrong way like in a chill breeze draft, Margaret's hair floating from her head like a Christmas tree angel's wings, still doing it but bracing and waiting, and then a stray step of the walking lightning came down through the top of the tree right by my back cabin door. It all happened so fast with the dog scrambling up on the bed and Margaret naked sliding off and the ceiling breaking open for a tree trunk like a telephone pole to come pile-driving all the way through and still on its way down into the floor.

And then it being quiet after the explosion, the tree trunk finally stopping, it smoking and smelling that blue electric smell with the burnt-up sap, me and the big-headed dog tangled on the broken bed, with Margaret having hit hard on her back near the hole in the floor stuffed with tree trunk, her long legs kicking in the air with a sexy view, an even more sexy view when I peeked over the mattress at her fully near the trunk of the tree, a sexy view that even further excited me about now being able to use a chain saw indoors.

But all wasn't just all right. When Margaret sat up she said Oh, like she had just thought of something she had forgotten, she pressed her fingers below her belly and then the lights flickered off and in the dark she said we needed to go into town for Della, Rusty's wife Della, Della who is what we have for a midwife and a cat-gut stitcher of slashed skin hereabouts. Della had delivered most nearby babies that could be gotten to, her delivering about two of her own with just Rusty's help.

All was not all right because to my eye Margaret wasn't showing that she'd had something of ours to carry, and the little quick-boil thunderhead seemed to be more of a front coming through with much of it still downriver letting lightning tall walk through trees. Even dressing in the dark, getting ready, not finding a flashlight that worked, I could tell there was lots of blood by the smell and by the way the dog was nervous. Even getting down to the canoe Margaret was feeling weak,

23

making it worse for her that the tide was out and I had to make two trips down to where the water was deep enough, one trip to drag down the metal flake canoe and the one trip carry her away.

Big rain like grapes hit us even before I pushed off in the dark, and the big-headed dog yelped and yowled at us from shore. The front moving in was coming at us right up the river bringing with it the turning tide and dirty chop. I couldn't see, not even Wolftrap Light, not even the number-four channel marker I used to reckon with. As I broke around and free of Stingray Point the breeze freshened harder so I figured best to hug inshore and make my crossing farther down hoping the wind would slack but it getting stronger and me figuring what was the right thing to do when I couldn't even see the bow of the canoe nor even Margaret wrapped in our fireside quilt laying quiet on pound netting in its bottom.

The rain broke harder, the canoe taking on some, waves licking the gunwales, my knees wetting, and a slosh around my ankles, me hoping the net would at least keep Margaret up a little out of it. Lightning was hitting something right regular over to south shore, and that was my only hope to see, when it lit the sky bone-white bright. I was pushing us as hard as I could with my best J-stroke but I could tell that not even did I pull my paddle out to dig for another stroke but what the wind pushed us back. I turned even closer to shore hoping for a break but not feeling it come.

Margaret shifted a couple of times pressing what we had for her to where the bleeding wouldn't stop, and even in all of it with her getting worse she shifted herself so not to disturb any headway I was making with the canoe, her maybe not really knowing I really wasn't making any. In a bright burn of lightning I slumped for a second seeing we still hadn't completely passed Stingray Point, and Margaret, lifting her head seeing it too, asked me to go ahead and talk to her, to tell her the story about Captain John Smith, and even though I had told her it a hundred times, not in that night could I remember a word of it, any more than I could turn us through the wind, so she told it, she told it like I had never heard it before, telling each part like it was a question, like how you tell a story to a child, asking with the sound of your voice, Are you straight on that part of the story yet? And then when she finished telling it she started telling it again until I started to remember it, and then remembered it well enough to tell her, telling her it, and also remembering too what that story is all about.

I paddled all night pushing back and across, making headway until just before light I was able to make the crossing where the river is a mile wide just up from town, where Rusty Shackleford has his half-fell-down dock. The light coming up was the kind that after a

25

front moves through gives everything a different color in the early morning break. The water sloshing in the bottom of my metal flake canoe had several different colors of blood in it, colors that were all over me and my legs from kneeling, colors running around my wrists like vines from where the skin had wrung off my hands paddling all night, colors black, dark red, and brown everywhere except in the quilt-tucked face of my Margaret, laying still on the net in the bottom of my metal flake canoe.

I don't remember much after, except seeing Danny Daniels Shackleford covering Margaret's eyes while pushing his fingers against his own, Scoop kneeling with us in the mud beside the canoe to straighten out the colored mess in his simple way but not being able to and going to fetch Della. I think I was there when the state people came and the sheriff came but I get hazy, maybe remembering fighting with someone over the fireside quilt they had unfolded Margaret from, maybe fighting with Rusty taking off my clothes with all the state people around, I think I did, and then I started walking the forty lengths of bad shoreline quilt-dragging naked to Where Lightning Takes Tall Walks, to where I've stayed just about all until today.

That must have been so many seasons I can't count ago. What they've caught a few sights of me since is mud covered in summer and quilt ragged in winter, being the haint the kids come to try to spook out at

night with their lights, me running clapping and splat-
tering through the mud when the quick-boil storms
come marching across the bay, me making to where the
tallest shortleaf pines grow, to stand as straight as I can
arms spread and face turned up, please begging for just
one long-legged kick of bone-white light right between
the eyes.

What I've come to see, though, is me laying lately
in deep holes dug in the woods, just outside of Rusty
Shackleford's town, and I've seen me slipping around
at night to where Rusty has my metal flake canoe
strapped to the rafters in the concrete-crate shed for
me to get when I want, and I've seen me creeping under
the back door of Rusty's five-sided store hungry to hear
a human voice or two.

And lately, I see me losing a taste for raw fish and
the young robbed from men's nets and animals' nests,
and I see me lonesome for that big-headed dog I see
sometimes sniffing at the tracks I've made at low tide,
tail wagging but too wall-eyed to think to follow the
scent, and me, I get to thinking about Stingray Point
and the story where they dug the grave but never the
man let them fill it, and I see today from my fresh hole
dug in the woods near Rusty Shackleford's town that it
must be Friday night with all the turnaround truck drivers drinking with Danny Daniels and Scoop, seeing how
young they aren't anymore, and seeing how many turnaround truck drivers are up against them, I figure just

as soon as that second bottle goes down and the fists come up, I figure I'll come down out of these woods swinging, putting in together with my friends, getting a fair knock of human life, taking a tall walk back into this town.

ON THE ROPE

I HAVE TO TELL MY UNCLE it is just a bread wrapper, a nothing piece of paper thrown up on the fence by the wind. I run out to show to him that that is all it is, but the spell is already on my uncle, and when I come back in from showing, it is just as well I should have stayed outside.

My gramere says the barge they brought down the bayou coming to get my uncle and his boat slid up on the edge of our backyard. She said the barge came gliding up soundless in the darkness with the floodwaters boiling under its squared bow, and she said God was giving her an eye of warning, showing her, See how that barge boils, like it is a man's head atop a pot the man

29

is boiling in alive. She said she could hear the water bubbling like it was hot and she said the way the flood churned beneath the bow it looked like the barge was coming even closer, but that it was only her will keeping it back, pushing it away from coming into our backyard and taking away my uncle and his boat.

Some men in green uniforms used a crane to hoist my uncle's boat up onto the barge. My uncle was afraid they would scratch the polished finish. Gramere said when my uncle came back from where the floodwaters had boiled away everything from the land my uncle did not care what the boat looked like. She said the boat looked like it had been whipped with wires, like it had gone on the barge and been whipped with wires, and my uncle looked like the men in the green uniforms had made him do it. She said the way my uncle was, was like when a man is drunk and whips a dog for no good reason and then when the man is sober he cannot look at it, even though he is a man and it is just a dog, that is how Gramere said my uncle could not look at his boat.

My uncle said at first when the barge stopped and the men in the green uniforms let his boat into the water he thought they had gone too far south, like the floodwaters had carried them all the way out into the Gulf. He said in the night all you could see was the amber light on the bow of the barge and all you could hear was the sound of the floodwaters boiling all around, boiling away everything from the face of the earth.

30

My uncle said all that night he drove his boat over the boiling waters wondering why the men in the green uniforms had put him so far out into the Gulf, until in the shine of his flashlight he saw an island of sparkling diamonds. When my uncle drove his boat over to the island he saw it was the crown of a tree boiling in the currents of the floodwaters and the diamonds were the eyes of all the snakes spun up through the branches. My uncle said the snakes dropped into the water so they could swim into his boat, but instead they were swept away into the darkness by the waters. He said after that he was careful of the islands and was not fooled again by their diamond-shining lights.

My uncle said that when the sun was supposed to come up it didn't come up at all, but just it started to rain harder. The rain got into my uncle's breath when he drove his boat. He had to hold his hand over his mouth like he was going to call a duck, but he was breathing in through the tube his fingers made instead of blowing out with his tongue. That was when the Brahma bull went by backwards. The way it went past, with just its head out of the water holding up its long, flat horns, my uncle said it looked like a big brown bird made of solid wood, gliding over the boiling waters for its breakfast. My uncle drove his boat alongside the Brahma bull and he looped some ski rope around the long, flat horns, but he said it did not work too well trying to pull the animal back to the barge because sometimes the ski rope pulled down on the Brahma bull's head so that its long, thin horns dipped into the water, and sometimes the Brahma bull's nose blew out water instead of breath, and by the time my uncle got over to where the barge seemed to be moving toward him, the ski rope was going straight down into the water by my uncle's boat like it held an anchor my uncle could not pull up. When the men in the green uniforms asked my uncle what it was, he said it was nothing, and he cut the ski rope loose from his boat and set out over the boiling waters again.

When it was supposed to be noon my uncle said he found the baby on the rope. He said it looked like somebody had tied a strong rope around the baby's waist and was still holding on, because the other end seemed deep down in the water. The baby was cutting through the current with its arms and head thrown back like it had just broken up to the surface to take a long deep breath that it was still taking. My uncle said when he pulled the rope from where it went deep into the water, it did not feel like it gave as much as it felt like it was being let go of. When my uncle got back to the barge with the baby on the rope, the men in the green uniforms gave him some coffee and a doughnut and a spam sandwich. He said the doughnut dissolved and the sandwich washed away and the coffee tasted like rain.

My uncle said the girl swimming on the barbed-wire fence had skin that did not come off in his hands like the skin on some of the others did. He said when he first saw her, her right arm was crooked over her head and her left arm was following, with her head turned like she was a swimmer in the boiling waters, making it look like she was stroking away from where everything was being boiled off the face of the earth. He said he was shouting at her, Swim, come on and swim! as he drove his boat over to her. He said even as he unstuck her from the barbed-wire fence he talked to her and looked away from her modesty, because her clothes had been boiled away, so he just focused on a little mark on her cheek like a snakebite the barbed wire had made that did not bleed because all her blood had boiled away, too. He made over her, protecting her modesty until they got back to the barge and the men in the green uniforms helped him hand her up from his boat so they could lay her on top of the other boiled-over people they had stacked at one end of the barge like corded wood.

My uncle said that after three days, when the only sun was just the amber light, the barge was full. The men in the green uniforms headed it back up the bayou, and even though sometimes they would see things hung up in the trees and caught along the fences they would not stop. The men in the green uniforms spread white powder out of green barrels on the people stacked under big green tarps. Men's boats like my uncle's were laid helter-skelter on the barge, all banged up like a lot of toys some bullies had come along and played too rough with. All the men like my uncle who had the boats stood around the edges of the barge away from the big green tarps, away from their boats they could not look at, and as far away from each other as they could without falling over into the boiling water. They stood watching for faces of boiled-over people to come up to just below the surface like they sometimes did, like they just wanted to sneak a peek before slipping back under. Then the men stood looking away to the trees and to the fences along the bayou that caught the boiled-over people. They stood looking, giving good hard long looks, because they knew, like my uncle knew, that once they were back up the bayou home they would never be able to watch a stew pot boil, or look at something caught on barbed wire ever the same again, even with someone like me coming in to show it is nothing but a piece of nothing thrown up on the fence by the wind.

HAPPINESS OF THE
GARDEN VARIETY

I FELT REALLY BAD about what we ended up having to do to Vic's horse Buster today, not that, looking back, all this could have been helped, all this starting when Steve Willis and I were ripping the old roof off of where we live in the shanty by the canal on Vic's acres. Vic was up to Norfolk again, checking on a washing machine for his many-childed wife, Steve Willis and I left to rip off the roof and hammer in the new shingles. We were doing this in change for rent. Every month we do something in change for rent from Vic. Last month previous we strung three miles of pound net with bottom weights and cork toppers. What we change for rent usually comes to a lot more than what I'm sure the rent is

35

for our four-room front porch shanty on the canal out back of Vic's, but Steve Willis and I like Vic and Vic lets us use his boat and truck for side business we do on new-moon nights.

Let me tell you something about what makes what we ended up doing to Vic's horse Buster all the worse. This is not to say about Vic less than Buster; me, I personally, and I know Steve Willis did too, hated Buster, Steve Willis having had to watch from far away Buster kill two of Vic's dogs. There'd be a stomp and a kick of dust and then a splash in the canal where it's a crab feast on old Tramp or Big Spot. Then there was Buster's biting and kicking of us humans, Buster having bit me on my shoulder once coming up from behind while I was scraping barnacles from one of Vic's skiffs in change for rent and then he didn't even move when I came at him with a sharp-sided hoe. Steve Willis had Buster kick in the driver side of his car door after Buster had been into some weeds Vic had sprayed with the wrong powder. Buster kicked in the door so hard Steve Willis still has to crawl in from the other way. It was this eating that finally got Buster in the end, though not being able to read the right powder label is something about Vic which made him have us around.

This is what I mean, this about Vic and about what we did to his horse to make things all the worse: Vic could not read nor write, and this about Vic affected the way we all were with him. What I mean all, means

Vic's wife and his children and Buster and his dogs and all the acres we all lived on down by the canal, and everything on all the acres, and everything on all those acres painted aquamarine blue, because one thing about Vic, and I say this to show how Steve Willis and I made this all the worse, was that Vic not reading or writing seemed to make him not to think about things like they had names that he had to remember by way of thinking that needed spelling, but instead Vic seemed to think about things in groups, like here is a group of things that are my humans, here is a group of things that are my animals, here is a group of things I got for free, here is a group of things I got off good deal-making, and here is a group of things I should keep a long time because I got them from some people who had kept them a long time, and maybe because of a couple of these reasons put together, Vic had another group of things painted aquamarine blue because he had gotten a good deal on two fifty-five-gallon barrels of aquamarine paint, and everything—even Vic's humans and animals who could not help but rub against or sit in somewhere because it was everywhere wet—everything was touched the color of aquamarine, though all of us calling it *ackerine*, because even spelling it out and sounding it out to Vic it still came out of his mouth that way, ackerine, keeping in mind here is a man who can't read nor write, and Steve Willis and I always saying it ackerine like Vic said it, for fun, because it also

37

always seemed like somehow we were always holding a brush of it somewhere putting it on something in change for rent.

So what made what we did to Buster worse were some ways in Vic's thinking which were brought on by him not reading nor writing. Just because somebody had kept Buster a long time to Vic made it seem Buster was very valuable, and even though the horse did come with some history tied to it, the real reason the people had Buster for so long was because they were old and could not seem to kill the horse by just shooting it with bird shot over and over even though they tried again and again, them just making Buster meaner and easier for Vic to buy when the two old people saw him in church and asked did he want a good deal on a historical horse. The history Buster had was he was the last of the horses they used at Wicomico Light Station to run rescue boats into the surf. To Steve Willis and I when we heard it said So what? but to Vic this was some history he could understand and appreciate, being an old sailor himself and it being some facts that did not have to be gotten from a history book that he could not read from in the first place.

What I came to find out later on was the heart tug Vic felt about this old horse that had to do with when Vic grew up, Vic's father having boarded a team of surf horses in a part of the house Vic slept in when he was a boy because all the children from Vic's parents spilled out of the two-room clapboard laid low in the dunes, not a far situation from Vic's own children who as long as Steve Willis and I have lived here I don't think I have seen all of yet because they keep spilling out of the house barefoot all year around and maybe it's because there are so many of them that Vic can't seem to remember all their names right rather than the fact he can't place in his mind what they are called because Vic cannot read nor write.

Anyway, the point I'm leading to about the heart tug is that where Vic spent his life as a child was sleeping with two other brothers in a hayloft over a team of old surf horses, and a hayloft mostly empty at that, not even because there was no hay to be had on an island of sand but because the team always grazed on the wild sea oats in the dunes, and this is what makes what we did the worse, this tug on Vic's heart to his younger days that Buster had, me hearing Vic tell it all to Buster one day when Vic didn't know I did, the feeling Vic remembered best of laying snug with his brothers, all of them laid all over each other to keep warm during the winter northeasters that shook the two-room clapboard and the tacked-on horse stalls where they slept, remembering them in the early mornings keeping warm wishing for breakfast while down below the horses would be stirring to go out, making droppings and the smell coming up to the warm, all-over-each-other brothers, the warm smell of wild sea oats passed through the two solid horses breathing sea fog breath.

So that was the heart tug Buster had and I don't mean to make Vic out strange owing to him liking the smell of an old horse passing gas, I think if you think about it there's really nothing there that doesn't fit with a man not thinking thoughts he has to read nor write, but fits well with a man who thinks of things as being good when they are human or animal especially if they came about by getting them free or from off a good deal.

I guess that is the main reason about Vic besides using his boat and truck on new-moon nights that Steve Willis and I stuck around, us in a couple of groups in Vic's mind mainly getting a good deal off of, us stringing nets, ripping roofs, and painting everything not breathing what we called ackerine, and that is also the main reason what we ended up doing ended up all the worse.

So like I said, this all started when Steve Willis and I were ripping the old roof off our four-room front porch shanty by the canal in change for rent. Vic had gone to Norfolk because he had heard of a good deal some people from church told him about to do with washing machines, and Vic, having stood in water barefoot while plugging his old washer in and getting thrown against a wall by the shock, naturally to his mind thought it was broken and in need of replacing. Vic had left in the morning coming in to get Steve Willis and I up around dawn to finish the roof and said only one other simple thing, the real easy thing, to please keep Buster out of the garden no matter what we did. Then Vic was off through the gate in his good-deal truck he had painted ackerine blue one night after supper the week before.

It was July hot, and before we started Steve Willis and I just walked around our shanty roof, just looking, because the island we live on is flat with just scrub pine and wandering dunes and from the single story up you can see Wicomico Light, the inlet bridge, and the big dunes where the ocean breaks beyond. It was a good morning knowing Vic's wife would come soon out bringing us some sticks of fried fish wrapped in brown paper, her knowing for breakfast we usually had a cigarette and a Dr. Pepper. For a long time Steve Willis and I had not made any new-moon runs to Stumpy Point to make us watch the one lane down to Vic's acres for cars we wouldn't like the looks of and I could look at Steve Willis and Steve Willis could look at me and we could feel good to be one of Vic's humans in a house on all of Vic's acres.

About midway through the morning after their chores about a half a dozen of Vic's kids came spilling barefoot out of Vic's ackerine blue house to ride the ackerine bicycles and tricycles and to play on the good-deal ackerine swing set and jungle gym. The older Vic's kids got to play fishing boat and battleship down on the canal dock as long as one of them stayed lookout to keep a count of heads and to watch for snakes.

From over my shoulder I was watching what Buster was up to. He stood looking up at me in the middle of the midday morning hot yard not seeking shade like even a common ass would but just standing in the yard near where the incline made of good-deal railway ties came out of the canal and led on up to the boat shed. Buster stood not even slapping his tail at the blackflies that were starting to work on Steve Willis and I up on the roof ripping shingles, but standing so still as if knowing not to attract one bit of attention to himself on his way to he and I knew where. I would rip a row of shingles and then look over my shoulder and Buster would be standing perfectly still not even slapping his tail at the blackflies or even showing signs of breath in and out of his big almost-to-the-ground-slouching belly. Just standing as if he was a big kid's toy some big kid was moving around in the yard when I wasn't looking, all the time moving closer by two or three feet at a time to the garden.

So I would rip a row and look, rip a row and look, never seeing him move even by an inch, and I saw Steve Willis was not even bothered by looking to keep an eye on Buster out of the garden even though Vic had told us both to do it, and the reason was a simple one for Steve Willis not to care, and boiled down, this is it: the evening Vic went over to make the good deal off the old people who had Buster for so long he rode Buster home and when he showed up at the gate needing one of us, me or Steve Willis to come down off the porch of our shanty to open the gate, it was me who came down to let Vic and Buster in the yard. That is the reason for Steve Willis not caring about Buster, not one thing more. Steve Willis stayed on the porch with his feet up on the railing watching Vic ride Buster by and me close the gate, and ever since, anything Vic tells us to do or about or with Buster, it is me who does it or me who listens even though Vic is telling us both, it is me and not Steve Willis, all from me getting down to open the gate that one time. That is why today Steve Willis was just ripping rows and not looking at Buster sneak, and I tell you, this forward thinking in Steve Willis when we make our new-moon runs, I like it then, but around the chores in Vic's back acres it can become tiresome and make you job-shy yourself.

Just about lunch time, just about the time for the little Vic's children to come into their house to get cold pieces of fried fish and Kool-Aid for lunch, the big Vic's children down by the dock all shouted Snake! and ran about fetching nets, poles, and paddles. This was a good time for Steve Willis and I to break so Steve Willis and I broke for a cigarette to watch what would all Vic's kids be telling around the table that night all supper long. Vic's big kids ran up and back the dock trying to catch the snake with their poles and paddles, and the poor snake swam from side to side in the boat slip with his escape cut off by one of Vic's big kids poling around in a washtub trailing a minnow seine. One of Vic's big girl kids caught the tired-out snake on the surface and dipped him out with a canoe paddle and one of Vic's big boys grabbed it up and snapped it like a bullwhip, popping its neck so it went limp. Vic's dogs that Buster hadn't yet kicked into the canal barked and jumped up on the boys playing keep-away with the snake until the boys took it up to the outside sink where we clean fish to skin it out and dry what the dogs didn't eat in the sun.

As they all paraded up to the house I came to notice the yard seemed even emptier than it should have been with Vic's kids and dogs all gone up to the big house, then I realized what piece was missing when between the wooden staked-out rows of peabeans I saw a patch of sparrow-shot ragged horsehair and a big horse behind showing out by the tomatoes. I shouted a couple of times and spun a shingle towards where Buster was at work munching cabbage and cucumbers but the shingle just skipped off his big horse behind and splashed into the canal.

By the time I got down from the roof leaving Steve Willis up there ripping shingles, Steve Willis not being the one to open the gate that first time Buster came to Vic's acres, Buster had eaten half the young cabbage heads we had. I knew better than to come up from behind a horse who can kick a full-grown collie thirty yards so I picked up the canoe paddle the big Vic's girl had used to fling up the snake on the dock with and went through the corn to cut Buster off at the cabbage.

But head to head, me shouting and making up and down wild slicing actions with the canoe paddle, Buster had no focus on me. Instead he was stopped in mid-chew. Then the sides of his almost-to-the-ground-slouched belly heaved out, then in, and then more out, moving so much more out that patches of horsehair popped and dropped off and I took a half step backward fearing for an explosion. I called for Steve Willis to come down, to hurry up, but all Steve Willis said was what did I want, and I said I think Buster is sick from whatever Vic had sprayed on the cabbage, probably not getting anybody to read the label of what it was to begin with, and then Buster side-stepped like he was drunk through two rows of stake-strung peabeans, and then he pitched forward to where I was backing up holding the canoe paddle, of little good, I was thinking, against an exploding horse, and then Buster, I swear before God, Buster erupt-belched and blew out broken wind loudly at the other end at the exact same time as his knees shook out from under him and he went down among the tallest tomatoes in Vic's garden wiping out the uneaten cabbage and some cucumber pickles too.

By this time Steve Willis had come down off the roof to look at the tragedy we were having in Vic's garden. It was hard to count the amount of summer suppers Buster had ruint and smushed. Steve Willis called

45

Buster a son of a bitch for wiping out the tomatoes, Steve Willis' favorite sandwich being tomato with heavy pepper and extra mayonnaise.

Steve Willis asked me did I hit Buster in the head or what with the canoe paddle but I promised I hadn't given him a lick at all with it, though we were both looking at how hard I was holding on to the handle. Steve Willis pushed in on Buster's big blowing-up belly with his toe and air started to hiss out of Buster's mouth like a nail-stuck tire, and the fear of explosion having not completely passed, we both stepped back. You could tell the little hiss was coming out near where Buster's big black and pink tongue stuck pretty far out of his mouth laying in the dirt between where the tomatoes were smushed and the cabbage used to be.

Steve Willis said This is not good.

Usually when Steve Willis and I have a problem in our on-the-side new-moon business, we say we have to do some Big Thinking, and we are always seeming to be doing Big Thinking in all our business, but since this was a Buster problem and since Steve Willis didn't come down off the porch that first time to open the gate, it was coming clear to me I would have to be the Big Thinker on this one. I stepped away to think really big about the tragedy, figuring from where the garden is situated around the boat shed by our shanty on the canal you can't see it from the big house. I figured I had a fair while to figure where to go with Buster after I got him out of the garden, hoping to find a hole enough nearby for such a big animal and do it all while Vic's little children slept out of the afternoon sun and while Vic's big children went to afternoon Bible study.

In the first part of thinking big I went up to the garage to get the good-deal riding lawn mower to yank Buster out until I remembered it had a broken clutch, and when I came back Steve Willis was holding back a laugh to himself, and I will say about Steve Willis, he is not one to laugh right in your face. He was holding back a laugh, holding the rope I'd given him to put around Buster to yank him out. Steve Willis asked me what kind of knot would I suggest he tie a dead horse to a broken riding lawn mower with.

I could see how far I could get Steve Willis to help with the Buster tragedy so I took the line out of his hand and put a timber hitch around one of Buster's hind legs saying out loud A timber hitch seems to work pretty well thanks a whole hell of a lot. I paid the line out from the garden and started to get that sinking feeling of a jam panic, a jam closing in needing Very Big Thinking, with not the July hot sun in the yard baking waves of heat making me feel any better at all. You get that sinking jam panic feeling, and I got it so bad that while I was paying out the line across the yard, and even though I knew I could not ever possibly do it, I stopped and held hard to the line and gave it a good solid pull the hardest I could to yank Buster out, straining, pulling, even when I saw when it was hopeless, and even with the jam panic worse, I had to let go of the line, and all the difference I had made was that now there was air hissing out from where blackflies were moving around and settling back beneath Buster's big stringy tail.

This was even better than before to Steve Willis who stepped behind what tall tomatoes were left so he wouldn't have to laugh at me to my face. I picked up a shingle I'd flung at Buster from the roof and spun it towards Steve Willis but it sliced to the right and shattered our side kitchen window and Steve Willis had to go behind the boat shed to laugh not in my face this time after you couldn't hear glass falling in the shanty anymore.

I gathered up the line bunched at my feet and trailed it over to the boat shed down to the dock. Vic's big Harker Island rig, our new-moon boat with the Chrysler inboard was gassed up with the key rusted in the ignition. I cleated the line that ran across the yard from Buster's hind leg onto the stanchion on the stern and shouted over to Steve Willis in the garden to at least help me throw off the lines.

I felt for an instant better starting up the big deep-throated engine so that the floorboards buzzed my feet, feeling the feeling I get that starts to set in running the rig over to the hidden dock on the south bay shore on new-moon nights, the feeling of the chance of sudden money and the possibility of anything, even danger and

death, and feeling now in a July hot sun the feeling of
Big Thinking a way out of a bad tragedy. With the engine running it was now possible in my mind that we
wouldn't lose our place of life in Vic's acres over something like letting a big horse die.

I was feeling better as Steve Willis threw off the stern
line and I choked the wraps on the stanchion leading
to where I could just see two big-legged hooves hung
up in the tomatoes where I could snatch Buster out and
decide what to do then, but the sound of the big engine
turning over brought out the dogs from underneath the
big house, them being used to going out with Vic in the
mornings to check five miles of pound net, and then
some of the older kids not yet set off for Bible study
started to spill out of the house to see what Steve Willis
and I were up to this time with their daddy's boat, and
if I looked harder at the house, which I did, I could see
the little Vic's children in the windows with diapers and
old Vic's t-shirts on wanting to follow the big kids out,
but not coming, them having to sleep in away from the
July hot sun.

Vic's dogs got down to us first, and even old Lizzie's
tan and gray snout, a snout she lets babies pull without
snapping, and a snout which would, when you were bent
over fooling with getting the lawn hose turned on, come
up and give you a friendly goose in your rear end, even
old Lizzie's tan and gray snout snarled back to show
ripping wolflike teeth when she saw that old bastard of

a horse Buster was down, and then she and all of Vic's other dogs were on the carcass and there was no keeping them away.

Now I had the problem of everybody in Vic's acres coming down to see what I had let happen to Buster, topped off by the dogs having their day going after Buster's body biting his hind legs and ripping away at the ears and the privates. The sight of the dogs on Buster was no less than the sounds they made, blood wild, and here came the rest of the kids to see all this, this even being better than chasing the watersnake around and out of the canal for a supper-table story.

I had to Big Think quick so I pulled Steve Willis by his belt into the boat, us starting over at that point about me and him and anything to do with Buster, forgetting that first time him not getting down to open the gate. I pushed forward on the throttle but did it swinging the bow off where I knew the sand bar was, still being in the right mind to know not to double up a dead horse tragedy with bad boatsmanship. When I rounded the dock and the line leading to where the pack of wild-acting animals were in the tomatoes with the horse carcass snugged tight, our bow rose and our stern squared, and I really gave the big old lovey Chrysler the gas and, looking over my shoulder, I saw Buster slide from the garden with still the dogs around, this time giving chase to the dragging legs, because in their simple minds they were probably thinking the only way to stop something with legs is to bite its feet whether that something is standing on them or not.

I knew that I was not just pulling Buster out of the garden now but that we had him sort of in tow, so that as we turned onto the canal proper and Buster skidded across the bulkhead and onto the dock that I knew wouldn't take his weight, I really had to pour the engine on, and I was right, Buster's big body humped the bulkhead over and came down splintering the dock we had just been tied to, but for an instant even over the dogs barking and the children yelling and the deep-throated throttle of the engine giving me any of anything making me feel better about all of this, just for an instant I heard Buster's hooves hit and clotter across the good-deal planking of the dock before bringing it down, and in that second of hearing horse's hooves on plank I had to turn back quick and look, because it passed over me that maybe I would see Buster galloping behind us giving chase to me and Steve Willis out of Vic's garden instead of us dragging his big dead body out to sea in tow.

We still had plenty of canal to cover before we broke out into open ocean. The dogs raced along beside us on the bank of the canal as far as they could but it was a game to them now, their wolf-like leaps mellowed out into tongue-flapping lopes. A couple of neighbors on down the canal came out to watch and the wake and spray from Buster cutting along ass backwards threw water into their yards. One of Vic's cousins, Malcolm, was working in a boat and seeing us coming he held up a pair of waterskis pointing to Buster laughing as we passed, but I could see open ocean so I throttled down and leaned hard forward to balance against the rising bow. I was glad I had enough forward thinking of my own to pull Steve Willis into the boat starting us over about Buster because I could look at him in the stern watching the big horse carcass we had in tow by a stiffed up leg, and looking at Steve Willis I could see it was sinking in on him that when Vic came home from Norfolk and threw me out of the back acres by the canal it would be Steve Willis himself being thrown out too.

I burned up about three hours of fuel looking for the right place to cut Buster loose. One problem we had was one time we stopped to idle the engine and pull up a floorboard so I could check the oil and while we set to drifting Steve Willis noticed that Buster floated. You could tell how the body was like a barrel just below the surface that it was the air or the gas or whatever was in Buster's big belly keeping him afloat. When I got up from checking the oil I threw to where Steve Willis was standing in the stern a marlin spike and he looked down at the spike and then he looked up to me like he was saying Oh no I won't punch a hole, and I looked back at him wiping the oil off my hands, looking back like Oh yes you will punch a hole, and when it came time for me to cut Buster loose out near the number-nine sea buoy and it came time for Steve Willis to punch a hole, I did and he did and it was done.

So here we are really feeling bad about what we finally ended up doing to Vic's horse Buster, us drinking about it in the First Flight Lounge after we called Vic's wife at home and she said Un huh and Nunt uh to the sideways questions we asked her about Vic being home yet, trying to feel out how bad was the tragedy, and her hanging up not saying goodbye, and us wondering did she always do that and then us realizing we'd never talked to her on the telephone before.

After we tied up Vic's rig in the ditch behind the First Flight Lounge we started to wonder if shouldn't we have let Vic had his say about what to do with his finally dead horse, so therein started us having the lack of forward thinking and of Big Thinking, and instead we were left to second guessing and after we had left the rig with its better-feeling hum and came in to drink, with the drink buzzes coming on ourselves, we started to feel naked in our thinking, especially when a neighbor of Vic's came in and shook his head when he saw us and then walked back out.

So what Steve Willis and I have done is to get down off the wall the tide chart and figure out where the most likely place for Buster to wash in is. We'll head out over there when the tide turns and wait for Buster to come in on the surf and then drag him up to take him home in a truck we'll somehow Big Think our way to fetch by morning. The tide tonight turns at about two thirty, just about when the lounge closes, too, so that is when we think we will make our move to the beach in front of the Holiday Inn, which is where we expect Buster back.

So Steve Willis and I sit in the First Flight Lounge not having the energy to begin to think about where we are to live after having to get ready to be kicked out of Vic's acres, much less having the energy to Big Think about pulling a sea-bloated horse out of the surf at two thirty in the morning. Here we are sitting not having the energy to Big Think about all of this when Vic walks in barefooted and says Gintermen, gintermen, another one of the ways he says things because he can't read nor write and doesn't know how things are spelled to speak them correct.

There is a nervous way people who don't drink, say, preachers, act in bars but that is not Vic. Vic sits at our table open-armed and stares at all the faces in the place, square in the eye, including our own we turn down. He sits at the table that is for drinking like it could be a table for anything else. Vic says he saw his rig tied up in the ditch behind the lounge on his way home from Norfolk, would we want a ride home and come get it in the morning.

Steve Willis and I settle up and stand to go out with Vic who says he's excited about the good deal he's come back with. Looking at Steve Willis I still see it's to me to start telling Vic about us having to wait for his favorite animal in his animal group to wash up down the beach, all at our hands.

Out in back of Vic's truck Vic runs his hands over six coin washing machines, something he does to all his new good-deal things to make them really his own. Vic says he got them from a business that was closing down, won't his wife be happy. Vic says our next change for rent will be to rewire the machines so they can run without putting in the quarters, what did we think. I start to tell Vic about Buster and the tragedy in the garden. I can't see Vic in the dark when they turn off the front lights to the First Flight Lounge but I can hear him say Un huh, un huh as I talk.

When I finish the part with Steve Willis and I waiting for the tide to turn Vic says Come on boys, we ought to get on home oughten we. All three of us sit up front of the truck riding across the causeway bridges home. All Vic says for a while is Well, my horse, my old horse, not finishing the rest, if there is anything to finish, and I get the feeling Vic is rearranging groups in his mind like his animal group things and his human group things and his good-deal-off-people things, and maybe making a new group of really awful people things with just me and Steve Willis in it.

But then Vic starts talking about how in change for rent Steve Willis and I are also going to build a laundry platform with a cement foundation and a pine rafter shedding, and Vic starts to talk like, even after taking rearrangement of all his things in all his groups, everything still comes up okay. Vic says oughten we lay the foundation around near the downside of the shanty where Steve Willis and I live so the soap water can drain into the canal, and after we figure how to put the sidings and braces up, oughten we put a couple of coats of paint on it to keep the weather out, maybe in change for some rent, and what color would us boys say would look good, and Steve Willis and I both sit forward and yell Ackerine! at the same time, us all laughing, and me feeling, crossing the last causeway bridge home, I'm happy heading there as a human in Vic's acres again.

THIS IS US, EXCELLENT

MY BROTHER GAINS HIS PORPOISE on my pony in
our race along the alleys home. I handlebar-heave
through some side-skidding garbage and hold him off
at the turn. I back-jam my pedals for my famous gravel-
scatter through our chain-link gate. I try to knee up fast
to do my Duke McQuaid sidesaddle dismount but my
toes catch on the crossbar and my brother slips in along
my side. Either on TV it's "Danger: Duke McQuaid"
or "Ocean Secrets," hundredth millionth. We elbow-
to-rib wrestle up the back cement steps. I punch my
brother in the boxwoods. I am pulling in the door.

I do the Duke McQuaid dive-from-the-back-of-the-
buckboard through the den door down in front of the

TV. The TV is already excellent, warmed up. My
brother claws the wall coming in off the kitchen and
surfs on the hall rug in on top of me. I'll break his wrist
in one snap for him to touch that dial. But what we've
missed coming in the alley the back way is our dad's
car out front with our dad home, and with our dad home
is our mom, backhanded backside down between the
coffee table and the sofa for company we'd better keep
our asses off of. What we've missed here is our dad
helping our mom up for another blap across the mouth.

This is excellent! I do the Duke McQuaid drag-away-
your-wounded partner with my brother, then we spin
out with toenail traction on Mom's Shine-Rite floors
down the hall to our room for shoes and shirts, leaving
it all, leaving on the TV, it having sports on it on anyway. So much sports on makes it less the chance for
our dad to have an interest in coming down the hall to
beat our asses. It's just our mom this time.

This really is excellent. Now we get to go snag a 'za
at Psycho Za, my brother and I getting to order the
Manic Size Train Wreck 'za with double everything hot.
We get two orders of Logjam Fries and two Gutbuster
SuperSodas, no lids or sissy sticks, please!

Our mom just has coffee to go with her Jesus homework. The lady next door brings the homework over to
her in little books. For us she brings usually some green
apples and some Christian outlines you can cut out of
God and the Apostles. My brother and I stick the cut-

outs in the spokes of our bikes with clothespins to rattle some clatter up and down our street until Mr. Murdock comes out and says, Stop it! He says, Here's a quarter for you and here's a dime for your brother, just, please, Stop it!

Our mom drinks her coffee cold, usually, not to burn the swole lip she has, the main reason for us going to Psycho Za. She sits while we eat and makes lines under the words in the little books the lady from next door brings over.

My brother and I have been snagging 'zas at Psycho Za when it was way before called Psycho Za, like the summer it was called Miss Romano's Pizza Palace, then Pizza Feast, then Earl's. When it was just Earl's I was little and my brother came in a sling and I would only have a soda or some snow cream and our beat-on mom just had cold coffee and cigarettes, no Jesus homework yet. Then our dad backhanding and giving our mom money for it after, I worked up through sodas and snow cream to pinball at Earl's, pizza burgers and playing with the knobs on the cigarette machine at Miss Romano's with my brother in a plastic chair, and finally us snagging some Manic Size 'zas at Psycho Za, leading to a ride on the Rocket Sling later in the park.

Talk about it, excellent! Sometimes on the ride my brother almost throws up the Train Wreck and sometimes he almost doesn't.

Then there are the nights when our mom calls up the

lady from next door to come over to Psycho Za and this is not real excellent. Some nights our mom's pencil points break and we don't have a sharpener in her purse. Some nights her coffee soaks through her Jesus homework and her split lip beats in hiccups against her bent tooth. On these nights my brother and I know not to breathe Train Wreck breath on each other or jerk on the cigarette coin return over and over for pinball quarters until somebody says, Stop! We just sit there and work over our food while the lady from next door works over our mom, pulling tissues and gold sticks of make-up from her secret-compartment purse. Sometimes, if it is something we should not see that she should do, she and our mom go back into the ladies' room for a long time, taking along the purse we are never left long enough with to go through. Whenever we can, we look in it, but mostly all we ever see when our mom's head is tilted back and the lady's back is turned, mostly only all we ever see over the Train Wreck down inside her purse is something looking like God or an odd Apostle.

What else is not real excellent about the lady from next door coming over to Psycho Za is that later she won't get in the Rocket Sling down at the amusement park with us. She just sits on the railing talking to the man with the cast on his arm running the ride. You should tell him, whoever he is, every summer different, about the way the clutch handle slips and breaks your arm. Usually it happens into the summer when the ride has been pretty good ridden and the handle starts to click like one of those piano clocks, back and forth, back and forth, until one night the handle wants to lie down flat against the place where the men running the ride like to rest their arm, waiting for the ride to be run. Every summer somebody different has it happen, it's just always the same kind of cast over the same kind of arms, arms like with amusement-type tattoos that look deeper blue in winter when you see them doing some job else, like taking out restaurant trash or reaching for cigarettes through bars in the windows of the jail downtown.

And the next-door lady not getting on the Rocket Sling means that our mom will not get on either. And even with our mom behaving at home so our dad has to blap her, still me and my brother have to have her for the feeling we get when she screams excellent, us spinning around, tucked under the metal bar that other people eating fried mess and French fries have greased up, the rocket cockpit like a chicken wire box you can see through, you can almost stick your finger through the wire and touch the two bolts that hold you on, that keep the rocket on the ride. First you go up rocking slow and you can study the painted rust in the cracks of the metal arms with the bulbs lit in between where they are burned out, and then up, turning heavy, the rocket cockpit sloping me against my brother and my mother, you can smell Train Wreck and coffee, the ride

61

taking your breath up until you spin around calm at the top at first, above our town and the ocean black ink you are on the edge of, and maybe a secret pinball quarter you were saving for yourself falls out of your shorts about now, you knowing the man running the ride can hear the silver bounce down while he watches in the sand for it to land, him waiting for it to rain change from people's pockets every time, like you wait all summer to show up and see his broken arm in a cast because nobody, even you, told him to watch out for that slipping stick on the clutch that starts and stops the ride.

And then, Down! you rocket-spin, going face first down. What you are seeing are just the bits out of a bigger thing, like when you and your best friend go through the trash behind the Ebb Tide Motel and find the instant camera pictures of naked people doing naked-people things, except when they get ready to go home from vacation they rip up all the naked pictures into the little bits you and your best friend find pieces of, hardly ever enough to put together, except for that one you don't even show your brother, the one of that fat lady with the scary titties, and how you keep one titty scrap and your best friend keeps the other, him also keeping the knees but you keeping what is real excellent scary, her happy face, you can see how funny she thought her vacation was with scary titties and sunburn.

So on the Rocket Sling you are seeing these little

pieces of the put-together picture so that when the ride really gets excellent spinning fast, mostly what you see are the spinning smears of the bulbs burning bright, and like ripped scraps, sometimes maybe you see the shoes of the breakable-armed man and sometimes maybe you see a far summer star, all the time smelling Train Wreck breath and coffee breath and breeze off the ocean ink where it's deep black night and scary because you can still look up and see the two rusted bolts that hold your rocket on and you think the bolts might break and you are going to fly right off the rocket ride arm, you are going to be slung right out of the park way out in the ink, all strapped down and locked in, to blub-blub sink without no one's reach, where nobody could ever possibly find you. That's the real excellent scary part, that feeling, and that feeling won't come if the lady from next door is there and your mom won't ride the ride, because what brings on that feeling most is when your mom rides wedged in tight with you and your brother on nights like this, when your mom will scream the excellent scream, the scream that people you see in snatches on the boardwalk stop and stare for, the scream that stops the ride next door, the scream that tells us to our hearts the bolts have finally broken.

My brother and I have been having off from school. Our mom won't let us go because of my black eye. I took it like a Duke McQuaid. I like to look at myself in the mirror and then spit in the sink like it ain't nothing to it at all.

We are at home alone so when we see the lady next door going up her walk my brother and I put our mouths up to the window shade and yell, Nosy Bitch! Then we lay down on the company sofa we're not allowed on and laugh. Our dad has said that Nosy Bitch was the one who called our school. They took us in the sick room and asked us was everything all right at home, did we tend to fall down and hurt ourselves. I told them our dad can beat up whoever he wants to. Nosy Bitch!

About an hour later that Nosy Bitch comes knocking at the back door while we're watching TV. We crawl in the cave behind the company sofa while the TV plays all the way up so I know she can hear it and I don't go to the door. I ain't coming out to face a rope around my neck, Nosy Bitch, you'll have to break down the door and shoot your way in. But she keeps tapping the glass like I know she won't go away until I go see, so I get up and go down the hall touching all the cousin pictures and then I make sure the toilet isn't running where my brother had been in there for about an hour and I take long linoleum slides in my socks across the kitchen floor and still I see her shadow on the curtain in back. It could be the shadow of a man with a loaf of bread under his arm.

It's just another bag of those green apples she's

brought us and a book of Jesus homework for our mom. She asks me, Is she here? and I say, Nah, she ain't here, and she says, Well, tell her I came by, and then before she leaves she looks over my head into the kitchen like she'd like to nose around in there so I close the door and watch her go back in her house through the shade.

Outside, me and my brother take some side-gnawing bites out of a couple of the green apples until we catch the Murdock cat in a run underneath some cars. We clobber him a few times with some apples to his brains until he makes a flat-eared dive into the storm drain. We see him down between the grates pushing against a ledge to keep out of the water so we chew some apples until they are the right size to throw through the grate. The cat has to swim away with apple mess all in his hair.

We make a few checks in the storm drain grates down the street but they run dry so I figure the Murdock cat has hit a turn in the pipe. We set back home when the mail truck stops and waits by a box while the mailman reads somebody's magazine. I line up for a shot like a bomb in a covered wagon but I'm off a little and the apple splits on the edge of the mailman's mirror and the mailman gets a face full of mess.

I don't do a Duke McQuaid. I run, pushing my little brother in front of me, pushing him so hard he starts to fall, then I grab him up before he does to push him

65

ahead some more. The mailman has dropped the magazine in the middle of the street to chase us. I try to run us towards home without really going there. I run us the direction of our house where I know whose fence is weak and where whose garage will lock. We turn the alley two people's yards up from our chain-link gate and I figure: the dark of the magnolia next door! I throw my brother over the black-rotted whitewash and angle myself through a pushed-in plank and that is where we see them.

In that place, so always shady and the dirt is always damp, under where the magnolia has knotted limbs and leaves like plastic, the breakable-armed man is dragging a rake towards where the lady next door is bent over a basket. They both have stopped in mid what they're doing to look at us, and I see that the man's arm is white without his cast, his skin has been shaded by it from the sun. There is a tattoo of Jesus I would recognize anywhere on his white-shaded arm. The face of Jesus is blue ink and the beard is roughed with the real hair of the breakable-armed man. The tattoo looks somehow excellent, a wanted poster alive from the TV show I want to be.

Storm has come and taken our power off so we look into my brother's eyes with a flashlight for any change. His eyes are still like when you are bored at home on

66

rainy days and you start to draw but you don't know
what to draw so you just draw a dot and then you circle
on and on the dot until it's a big black hole in the middle
of the paper.

All around my brother's sick bed made up on the
company sofa with a sheet and a pillow are stand-up
Christian cut-outs of God and the Apostles. We have
two of one, the one with the sheep up his sleeve. Our
mom has made the green stuffed chair the place where
she prays for my brother and waits in the dark with the
flashlight.

Our dad is out in the car listening to the radio scores
because the power is off to the TV. We know not to
bother him. This afternoon Mr. Murdock came over and
then my father grabbed me by my belt and collar like
to clean a saloon bar with. I was lucky. When I hit by
the TV I didn't taste blood or anything and when he
came over I knew to stay down and just study his shoes,
to just watch for the toe parts to swell, to get ready for
him to bend down and pick up my head.

For my brother it was a simple palm-push but my
brother's head was too close to the wall. I have told him
a hundred million times to stay away from the walls
even when the walls make corners. He was too close
so when his head got pushed it sort of bounced off the
wall and back to our dad's palm like to kiss it, and then
he fell out on the floor like a girl on the playground
having a spell.

There is brought-over apple pie from next door smelling up the kitchen. Before the storm the breakable-armed man was in the neighborhood looking down into the storm drain grates. He had both hands around the bars and was kneeling over them like a man in a face-down prison.

From the window where I sit near my brother I can hear Mr. Murdock calling his cat. The radio plays out in our dad's car. In the dashboard lights I can see his outline like a backwards Christian cut-out. A candle is lit in the window next door. For as long as you look at it, it never flickers.

This is us, excellent, a family night out. Not even have we not had to go to Family Fish House to eat but we've come to Psycho Za to snag! Our mom has her hair fixed and has on the too-big red plastic parka with our dad's name on the front. Our dad has said for us to have anything we can think of we want on the list of things to eat. What I'd usually do is split the Manic Train Wreck with my brother but he is still acting funny about eating and stuff, like he's not all the way woken up and his eyes are like old fish-tank water. When he cries it's more like a hiss, like how a soft knife sounds when you split a green apple open.

Our dad has wads of quarters in his pockets for me and my brother to play pinball but my brother leans in the booth against our mom with his dead eyes while our mom pets his hair and our dad watches our car in the parking lot for somebody not to break in and steal it. There are still stacks of quarters when our food comes so I know I can tilt and push the pinball harder.

I eat my Brainbuster Burger heavy on the Super Goop and dig around in the catsup puddles with a Terminal Case of Logjam Fries but everyone else doesn't look down at their plates, like the food isn't good enough to eat. The family-night-out meal comes and goes with just me working on the platters, and then we get up and I show our dad where to pay while he strums quarters in his pockets and then we all stand out by the newspaper racks in front of Psycho Za like nobody knows where we are or which way home.

I see this is excellent so I say Rocket Sling! Rocket SLING! and our mom looks at me and says, It's too late, way too late for the Rocket Sling. She says, It must be closed, and my brother mashes his face on her pants leg. Our dad says, Everybody get in the car.

I think at first our mom is right when we see the park shutting down with canvas wraps over the kiddie boats and there's just an ice cream crowd through the gate coming out. The more our mom says, No, the more our dad turns his fingers on her arm to lead us in.

This is excellent! Just us and the Rocket and the breakable-armed man. He is changing lights on the metal arms from a box of white sleeved bulbs. He comes down climbing off the gears and hitches up his pants. He opens a rocket cockpit and he does it in a way to make us feel that if he had a watch he would look at it because it is late. The boardwalk is empty, the Roll-Go-Round next door is dark.

Our mom would no sooner get us in the rocket. My brother has his face in her pants zipper. She says, Please, to our dad. Our dad steps into the rocket and his weight works on the bolts that hold him on overhead. We stand by the ramp and wait. Come on, he says, we're going all the way tonight. He waits and we wait and then he starts to climb out to pull us in so I step up but the breakable-armed man moves faster and I watch his tattoo arm bring down the bar across our dad and snap the cockpit shut. I am still close as he slips in the clutch to bite a gear and our dad rocks a bit, porch-swinging, before the bolted-on arm lifts his rocket slowly to the top.

With his lopsided weight on the empty ride, the steel arms bend and bounce his one slow spin down, and in the bottom light I see a white-knuckled grip around the greased metal bar. Up he goes, his outline at the top before he rockets slung out full, to fall faster where we stand. The breakable-armed man leads us around behind the waiting line railing and then he drifts off backwards like as soon as he is in the dark he will run all the way home.

We are left alone in all this light. The bulbs running past throw shadows, the gears gnaw themselves against the motor. We cannot move to stop or move to go. We can only watch from behind the bars of the railings as around and around and around the rocket with our dad spins in perfect catching ups and perfect catching downs until there is the sound of metal breaking free. Something zings by my head like a bullet on TV. Things are starting to shake apart, things are coming loose, pieces of metal are rattling around the rockets and are being spun out of the light into the ink slapping the beach behind us.

Our mom takes a step towards where the breakable-armed man should stand. She has to drag my brother. He is green-apple screaming. We can hear more pieces falling as our dad rockets past. I look at the clutch handle I would never go near in a hundred million years. It is vibrating so fast it is a blurring thing in two places at once.

I see Dad up, I see Dad down. Breaking-loose metal hits against our clothes and we shield our eyes with our arms. We can't look and we can't not see what will happen next. I see something else and it is excellent, in the outline of Dad as he is slung up, still for a quick, quiet second before he is slung back down, and down I see him see the scrap of me, and then up I see his outline, his arms grabbing at the air and spreading space, and then down I see from his pockets the busted wads of silver sling into the sand, and then up I see him excellent, snatching in the dark at the things that will fall to our feet from heaven.

THE ICE AT THE BOTTOM
OF THE WORLD

BILL DOODLUM WAS HOME FROM THE HIGH SEAS,
having all the holidays he missed at once. Powell was
over early. Louise Doodlum was just taking up Bill's
plate of birthday breakfast that he missed coasting
south through the South China Sea.

So, how was Antarctica? Powell asks Bill, warming
him up for what lay ahead, and Bill says, Hot! We go
in their summer, he says, for the ice to break up. Louise
Doodlum looks at Powell over Bill's shoulder with what
is left of the birthday breakfast, the toast rims, the
chicken legs, the blue potato gravy. Powell knew how
he came out around Miss Louise, always being That
Man, like, That Man this and That Man that, like, Lisa

Lee, how can you have it up in you to let your car be
seen in front of That Man's trailer home so early Sunday
mornings, with Tommy John around and what people
say, Miss Louise not to Powell's mind giving him any
credit for in fact being the one whose hands shake and
throat bobs at the whine of the downshifted Suzuki,
missing sleep, listening through Lisa Lee's snore for
her husband's motorcycle outside his door. Powell looks
the look back to Miss Louise until she shakes the birthday plate into a paper sack in the sink.

There's a desert there in summer, with sand as brown
as your boots, Bill tells Powell. And they got the comical
penguins. Bill says, You can lay over the ship's rail
looking over at them on the ice in your morning shirtsleeves, them diving and flapping until a killer whale
rushes up from beneath, flipping the ice cake and tum-
bling the birds down the fish's big open throat. Bill says,
It's all real comical.

Miss Louise starts bump-sucking the vacuum around
the men's feet. Bill says, Come on in the front room,
let me show you what else.

Even being July third, the day before the Fourth, the
Doodlums have set up in their front room a white plastic
bristle-branched Christmas tree hung with red balls and
sitting on top a tinfoil angel, Styrofoam-headed with
blue sequin teardrops pinned into its white bubbled
skull. Laid around the tree is the Christmas left over
from the day before, the Christmas Bill missed laid up

in Bombay next to a phosphate freighter. Spread like it had been jerked from the box once and left thrown was a blue silk kimono from China for Miss Louise that even Powell could see that unless somebody would cut Miss Louise in half she would never fit into. For Lisa Lee was a five-foot stuffed kangaroo from Fremantle, Australia, showing a runway smudge where Bill had fallen down drunk with it the length of the airplane steps, Lisa Lee telling Powell how quickly, not even having seen Bill for months, Miss Louise had spun right around right then to wait in the car, and how the stewardesses were surprised at the age of the intended daughter for the gift from the way Bill had talked about her, the only daughter to help her daddy up, Bill having flown the kangaroo beside him first-class and buckled up to Norfolk, Virginia, from Rota, Spain. For Claudia, home from art college up North, was a hand-carved ivory polar bear pulling a sled of six men and a dog. Bill could not remember right away from where it came.

What Powell felt the most uncomfortable with was the antique brass-barreled long musket from the Persian Gulf Bill had brought for Tommy John's gun collection, Tommy John, the husband Lisa Lee had when Bill set off the year before around the world. Powell held it, sighting outside on Miss Louise getting in her car. Powell wondered whether the parts it needed to fire could be bought nearby or not, when Bill said, I'd cry about it too if I was you. Powell begged pardon. Bill said, The Christmas angel, the one crying blue tears. Bill said he'd cry too with such an ugly tree run up his rear behind in the middle of July. It's a joke, Bill said, a Christmas family joke. Powell smiled, pumping air hissing through his teeth as much as seemed required; then they turned their backs and took their leave of all the left-open gifts left over from the Christmas missed around the world.

What Powell was over to ask for was Lisa Lee's hand, second hand as it was, a little legal holdover from the mixed-up divorce-from-Tommy-John papers nobody had signed correctly and everybody did not want to sign again. Powell and Lisa Lee knew a magistrate to straighten it out. People on the outside said to Powell, People don't do that any more, the hand-asking, and what Powell said back was, Yes, you do do that in Doodlum County, slim as this finger bit of marshland is into the Bay and as fickle as it is by its connection with the world at George Doodlum Addison's whim to swing the drawbridge back and forth to let you on or let you off, to keep you in or keep you out. You do that when you don't share a carved name at all in the cemetery you have never set foot in for fun, spite, grief, or all three.

Powell thought it was convenient that half his trailer home living room wall was papered over with old *National Geographic* maps to hide where the dartboard used to be. He had charted pretty well Bill's coming home, because back around the world, when Bill was sailing south of a smushed mosquito was when Powell decided to ask for Lisa Lee's hand. From then on Bill was a tag of electrical tape in Bombay, with Lisa Lee leaving earrings on the dresser, and Bill was a stick-on gold star from Lisa Lee's second-grade deportment book stuck in Antarctica about the time Tommy John returned her hope chest swinging from the hook of a tow truck, and set-to-fly-home Bill was a big red thumbtack stuck in Rota, Spain, with Lisa Lee cutting wedding-dress patterns. Powell saw no need to pencil in Bill's flight over the Atlantic Ocean. We are where he will be next, he said.

With Miss Louise outside and gone in her car up to the church hall to staple paper to the picnic tables for the Fourth, Bill took Powell into the garage to see what else from around the world and to check the long-necked beer and soda pop chilling down in the walk-in. In the garage with the walk-in was Lisa Lee's hope chest, just like it had been winched down off the tow truck by Tommy John, and right alongside was Bill's footlocker sea chest shipped in from him coming in home off the high seas. The feeling of sheer weight Lisa Lee's chest gave off and the banged-around, still-bolted-shut look of Bill's gave the chests the look of two pieces of unclaimed cargo freight you sometimes see left around the docks that when you finally do open only have in them rusty scrap iron pieces of something odd wrapped in ragged burlap and felt.

77

Bill handed Powell a cold long-necked beer, and even though it was fairly well before noon Powell felt he would be in this for the duration to try his question so he took it. From his khaki ship's captain pants pocket Bill pulled a tiny shackle key ring and set to work popping the locks on his long footlocker sea chest. Powell considered that from Bill's clothes maybe yes, you could tell he had something to do with ships, but in general maybe you would think he stitched canvas or counted stores. A short man, his shrunken-back skin was pale and pearly, shielded from the sun by Plexiglas shades on the bridge of his ship. The thick lenses of black glasses made his eyes look as if they were watering, ready to cry at any time, and in his posture he was a little bent over, maybe from the clutching pain of one lung already removed, the lung punctured in the Pacific he got the medal for, braced on the fantail of a sinking ship with a clustered crowd of Doodlum boys like himself, still firing handguns and carbines up at the diving Japanese until there was nothing left to shoot and no one left to save except himself and a cousin, shot through the lung as the ocean sucked their ship swirling from beneath them, this little stooped-over man with the teary eyes and the trembling hands.

Bill was opening the sea chest to show Powell what else from around the world when Duchess, the Irish setter dog, bobbed her gray-snouted red head in the frame of the garage door, her wet matted hair hung with thick fingers of mud from chasing seagulls in the low tide. Come 'ere, Duchess, Bill said, but Duchess just looked a little stupidly back and then trotted away even with Bill calling Duchess, Duchess. It has been the same with dogs and kids for twenty-six years, Bill said. No one knows a come-home stranger. Bill started again to dig through the dirty folded-over khaki shirts, bringing up the smell of sour aftershave and, somehow, hot linoleum. Louise says she's only seen me less than half the married life we've had, said Bill, reaching deeper in his locker for a small case like a toolbox. Me, I can look at it in a different way and see it as just being half-married. Half-married, said Bill again. He said, Can you think about that? and Powell, sitting on Lisa Lee's hope chest, said that he probably could.

Bill unwrapped a pistol out of a greasy leather rag from the toolbox. Be careful now, it's loaded and I never have the safety on, Bill said. Feel the balance and the grip, it's Italian with a nine-shot clip. The company gave us guns last year against those boat people in the South China, he said. You don't know but lots of them are pirates. This pistol is my personal choice, he said, slipping back the slide action.

The gun discharged in Bill's hands, putting a hole in the riding lawn mower.

Don't worry, Bill said, I've got extra ammo.

Powell was sorry he had let the talk slip away from being married, but he had been thrown off by the half-married remark. But what really surprised Powell about Bill was the trained quick pull and draw of those watery-looking eyes behind the thick lenses of the black glasses that Powell studied as they talked, eyes sensitive to detect the extra shade of dark in the glittery silver seas, eyes even able to see a hardly appeared slice of fin in sharp peaked chop or a quick dip of waterspout twelve miles out in a closing dusk. Here the bastards come, Bill said, sounding surprised. Look at how they are coming.

They were two jets, two flattened specks on the horizon coming so right on they seemed to swell with speed, two tiny black triangle heads over the channel and lower than the trees on either side, two heads with swayback trailing plumes of exhaust, dirty brown fumes already shifting sideways on the breeze behind so they approached like sidewinders on the silver path of water, heading so straight on into Doodlum County, making their weekly practice run on the drawbridge where George Doodlum Addison sat looking down into the cars passing underneath, hoping for a shot of hem-hiked leg, or, if he was lucky, a peek down Claudia Doodlum's sundress she always puckered open for his pleasure; here they came, approaching at a speed faster than the sound they made, so that all you thought you could hear when you saw them coming was the empty air in the seam of light they were splitting to get to where you stood until they would be long passed overhead when the steady leaving roar would follow the explosion so quaking that in the Doodlums' den there was a crack running down the far wall in the shape of the California coastline that inched a pinch farther down every week they flew. Here they came.

Bill was out on the end of his dock with his toolbox, digging and putting together like a military drill a short-stocked thick black pistol with a breeched barrel big enough to accept a cartridge the size of a soda can. Don't stand directly behind me, said Bill when the jets were about six seconds away, and Powell did not.

The jets were so low their exhaust boiled in the tree-tops just as Bill fired his piece. The thing going off like a firecracker in a paint can was the first blast in a chain of explosions that included two sonic booms and a sound that sent Bill and Powell running into the garage to spend the rest of the morning drinking long-necked beers behind locked-shut doors, sometimes leaning to look out the windows a little to the north and a little to the south, one way to check for the Navy to come and the other expecting Miss Louise and a carload of women wired up on double-octane church caffeine coming over for a lunch of peanut butter–fig preserve sandwiches like Miss Louise had said they would.

Bill smoked one-after-another cigarettes, working the side of his chest, pumping one-lunged smoke streams, saying he had only thought a flare would scare the jets off, honest to goodness, he said. Powell said he was sure they would have heard a crash if there had been one after the jet engine sucked in the flare, and Bill said maybe not, not if the jet had headed right out over the ocean. Powell said there wasn't even a sign of a parachute, just that horrible grinding noise they heard for a long, long time. It had rained shredded motor metal confetti in the field across the road. If we can stand it until tomorrow, Powell said, maybe we'll see in the paper if the Navy is missing a jet or not, and Bill said HAH! to that. Bill said he knew firsthand how two years before a jet had run off a runway in Virginia Beach blowing up a lady in a station wagon going by, with the two pilots hanging by their straps in a tree with no heads on, having gotten them lost during ejection. Bill saying the Navy cut off all the roads, and the next day where it all happened was nothing but a plowed-under ground with a man riding a tractor laying in rows of peanuts with nothing in the paper. All in one night, Bill said, opening two more long-necked beers.

They sat in the dark garage, Powell on Lisa Lee's hope chest and Bill on his own, sometimes leaning out the windows to look a little while north, and then a little while south. What did exactly it sound like to you? Bill asked Powell. Powell said he didn't know, but at first it was like somebody running a giant vacuum cleaner that sucked up something like a bottle cap but heavier, more like a fifty-cent piece, except it was a sound loud enough to hear for ten of fifteen miles.

Powell said, What about you, Mr. Doodlum? and Bill said Call me Bill. Bill said, It is a funny thing about sounds, what a sound will push up out of you like something squeezed from a blister. Bill pulled two more beers from the walk-in. He said, You know Louise is a Carter from Carter, you know about twelve miles up the river, and Powell said Yes sir, he knew that, knowing there were only two counties, Doodlum County and Carter County. Bill said before he and Louise were married her father started the sawmill at the river headwaters, floating logs on barges up and lumber back, back down to Norfolk and up around to Baltimore. Powell said yes, he knew where the pulp mill was, and Bill said, Yes, but this was way before that. This was when not even all the logs came up the river but that Kirby Carter was still cutting out the virgin woods, trees four and five men thick around the trunk. Trees so big Kirby Carter had brought down from Canada by barge a five-and-a-half-foot buzz-saw blade with a stripped-down steam locomotive to drive it. It took two weeks working around the clock to set it up getting running right, and ever it started spinning it only stopped for two things, one for filing the six-inch teeth with hand rasps and oil. Bill opened the side garage door to wet down the azaleas.

Kirby Carter, Bill began again, brought in Pamunkey Indians to run the saw at night for half wages. And on nights was when Kirby Carter had Louise there, mostly alone, to go in and refigure the books in Kirby Carter's favor. Oh yes, said Bill, our Louise fixed the books for her daddy, never looking back for it that I know. But what else of it all was that, though don't look at her now, Louise was all we had for the best-looking girl around, and with her dark-complected, she stirred the Indians, like every net dragger, lumberhand, and boat builder alike, crazy with her looks, but only them around with her alone, working at night for half wages.

Bill lit another cigarette and side-smoked it one-lunged.

So, Bill said, I would court her Friday and Saturday nights over in Carter and she'd ride over with her sister Sundays for church over here. It would be the weekdays in between, Bill said, that no matter how blessed tired I was from pulling net or lifting tongs on my father's boat, I'd lay upstairs in this very house all frisky-feelinged and blue over Louise. You see, we didn't have all the liberties you take today, he said to Powell, and Powell took his point.

Bill sipped his beer, looking, leaning out the window a little south and then a little north.

You see, Bill said, I also knew the Indians drank on the all-night shift, not a lot to be fired over on half wages, but enough so'd one or two a year would lose a hand or at least a set of fingers. So you see, I'd lay sweat-bothered and blue twelve miles downriver from Louise every night no matter how tired, getting no sleep, I'm telling you, listening to the gottdamn tide come in and go gottdamn out, worrying about those gottdamn Indians around my Louise, you know, like you're on the edge of a bad sleep, until it was time to go out again with my father in his boat. I tell you that was backbreaking work to get tired over too, work like no one really has to do any more, I'm telling you, and Powell said, Yes, sir.

So you see at night, with the Indians a little wet and, to give them their due, working under strings of bare bulbs lit dim from a generator, hardly enough light to see by but drawing every itch and biting bug around, maybe one of the Indians would chain-lever a log on the belt set for the big buzz-saw, and maybe in the bad light he wouldn't see where somebody'd left a come-along spike in, or maybe he'd be too busy slapping bugs to see where the tree had grown so big it had grown all around a rock the size of a loaf of bread like a tree will do, and maybe the saw would plane off a plank or two before the steam-drive six-inch teeth would try to bite into solid steel or native stone, but then the sound would be out, out from under the open-sided shed where the buzz-saw bit. And let me tell you, they couldn't shut that saw down fast enough to stop that sound from rousing six miles overland Kirby Carter pajama-ed on horse-back, or to stop that reaching screech of a kind of sound like we heard today, they couldn't stop that sound traveling twelve miles downriver to where I lay on the edge of a bad blue sleep over Louise, and don't you know what that sound reached me as, on my sweat-wetted bed, it reached me as Louise screaming my name for help from all those gottdamn Indians. That was a sound, son, that truly traveled your ten of fifteen miles, that sound.

Bill and Powell were quiet a long time, turning up their long-necked beers and listening to the foam settle back to the bottle bottoms.

I think I married her because I couldn't take that sound any more, said Bill. The war started, the sawmill burned, and I've been gone almost ever since.

They seemed to be getting to the end of something, even if it was just the case of beer. Powell had had so much to drink that his questions about love and marriage were just echoes in his head of a thought he could not remember. Bill beat his foot against the sea-locker side. Forget what I said about only being half-married, he said. I got a wonderful wife, I got a wife like all men should have, a wife the kind who will either make you or break you a place in this world.

Bill stretched back on his sea chest like a body out of its box. I just now see that I am finally home, he said.

Powell left the garage, looking a little north and then a little south, leaving Bill asleep inside, sleeping the kind of wheeze snort snoring sound a man with one lung makes.

· · · · · ·

In the winter later, Powell stood wanting beneath a sky that was a blue-pearl boil frothed in off-white slices that came down out of the morning fog as dirty-feathered seagulls in their turns. The white mists of foggy plumed tongues fell the few feet between heaven and earth and licked at the crystalled fingers of early snow fallen in Doodlum County Christmas week, unusual. Powell stood wanting with his wife at the left-open broken place in the ground made for the later laying in of Bill Doodlum. The grave-digger's shovel had flung a few spare spades of brown sandy soil beyond the green canvas catch-tarp, making tiny desert valleys in the mountain landscapes of ice.

In Powell's coat pocket was the empty nine-shot pistol, Bill Doodlum's personal choice, the one Louise Doodlum had called Powell to come over and fetch from her, she said, come fetch what she had put Bill Doodlum out of his less-than-one-half-lunged misery with, her calling when Powell and Lisa Lee were sitting around their trailer-home kitchen table cutting out commas, colons, and question marks for Lisa Lee's grammar class. I did it like he said, careful not to bounce the bullets off the oxygen tank so to blow up hurting anybody, Louise said to Powell, as with a top and bottom hand movement he slipped the pistol away from how she still held it when they arrived, slipping it away as gently as he would have a mitten from a sleeping child's curving hand.

Upstairs, Powell pushed open Bill's bedroom door. Bill was listing to his left off a cloud of pillows, his left arm and hand a little over the sideboard edge of the bed, as if he had awoken with a sudden thought and was reaching for his slippers on the floor. His pale blue pajama top was to Powell a reckless spread of red punctuation, mostly periods and an exclamation. In the gunsmoke smell of after-violence, Powell sensed a building modulation in the room counted off by the clicking bedside clock and the steady hiss of oxygen. At first calming, its sudden familiarity to Powell as sounding like something about to explode urged him back downstairs.

In the kitchen, Louise and Lisa Lee held each other like wrestlers in a headlock, the thick-wristed arms run up under each other's same-waved hair and down over the same muscle-wound shoulders, faces in necks talking and fronts not touching. Powell sat at the telephone table in the den watching the two women in the slice of kitchen light, they having already gotten out on the counter the tough steel four-legged five-gallon coffee-maker indefinitely now plugged in for days. Powell pulled the telephone into his lap, thinking who to call, still studying the two women in the wrestlers' embrace in the kitchen light. These two women, each in their time the closest thing to best-looking the county had, Bill had said, they both with the up-jutting bows of sharp, swelled breasts and the high rounded sterns ex-

actly built like the workboats in the Bay needed nearby
for local waters, boats that bore the names of the captain's wives, even out there a *Lisa Lee* and a *Miss Louise*
from a former husband and a forties flame, the form
inspirational and practical, the wide wrists and sturdy
legs to keep paint on the houses, to shore up the barns,
to wrestle machines that turn the soil and cut the hay,
machines that broke down always when the men were
gone to sea, the same time as everything else, gone
when babies were born, houses burned, cars collided
with Doodlum children beneath and at the wheels, the
highway patrol saying, What do you expect from children left to run wild with the daddies sending sometimes money from Taiwan or Tel Aviv or a telegram
dictated in drunken, divided words, saying, STRAIGHTEN
UP BACK HOME, YOU, these daddies, these husbands
bringing gifts back ten years too late to matter, these
women cheated by half-life marriages to half-married
men, strangers always coming home, drinking, restless
to return to sea, to some little empty bleak strange strip
of desert sand in the ice at the bottom of the world,
while these women shouldered it all, the everything
else, all on those thick-muscled shoulders and sturdy
legs Powell admired from the telephone table in the
den, Powell holding the telephone in one hand and the
pistol in the other, still wondering who to call.

Doc Mackenzie said he had Perry Como on the TV,
the Christmas special, was it an emergency? Powell

said no, it didn't seem to be an emergency, but there seemed to be some circumstances. Doc Mackenzie asked would these circumstances bring Bill Doodlum back to life? and Powell said no, these were more like family circumstances, and Doc Mackenzie said oh, all right, he would pack his bag next commercial break.

Doc was a sideways Doodlum like Powell, that is, marrying high into the family but on somebody's secondhand time around. For Doc, it was a Hudgins Doodlum off a golf pro in Richmond at the country club where he used to play, Mary Beth Hudgins Doodlum Walker Mackenzie now. Doc had done the Doodlums a favor because, like bouncing genes in the Doodlum clan there were women like Lisa Lee's own sister, Claudia, who had certain notions, especially after spending some time up North like Mary Beth and Claudia both had, and if Doc had not stepped in when he did to marry Mary Beth, she said she would have gone ahead with her plans to turn her corner of Doodlum County, inherited as potato fields, into a high-walled playground for her Richmond friends to come and sit in the sun naked, playing cards, but Doc gathered up what he called her loose ends, so that mostly what she did now was paint, on pieces of weathered potato-shed siding, picture after picture of seagulls circling Wolftrap Lighthouse, the same pictures in every Doodlum home, piles of which show up unsold year after year at the Fourth of July bazaar, Doc not getting much credit for his stepping in although the county did need a doctor, taking even one from Richmond, Richmond not being all that far away, but to people used to distant ports and postmarks, Richmond could as well have been Rangoon and just as foreign too.

Doc said, standing beside Bill Doodlum's bed, that he was surprised Bill did it not having finished the paperback thriller on the nearby table with a bookmark in a place about halfway through, and Powell said that was part of the circumstances he wanted to talk about, that Miss Louise had . . . but Doc cut him off sharply and said, Son, do I look that ignorant to you? Doc said, I can count eight or nine holes here, any one could have been the only one Bill needed. When I say what I say about him doing it, in my mind and in what I write down he did do it, whether this suffering man pulled the trigger or not. Then, sounding like his raised voice would waken Bill, he said to Powell, Son, this is a suicide under what you yourself said were family circumstances. You didn't call the sheriff, you called me. What does that tell you to yourself?

Powell looked down at the pistol he was still holding.

Doc sat down hard on the bed, shifting Bill almost over the edge before Doc pushed him back onto the pillows. Bill did this, said Doc. Call Claudia so she can get a head start home and then call the sheriff. I'll go down and see to Miss Louise. Leaving the room, Doc pulled the bookmark from the pages of the bedside pa-

perback thriller, losing Bill Doodlum's place in it
forever.

Powell called Claudia, already overdue down from
art college for the holidays. Powell called the number
three times to make sure it was the right one, and each
time before the leave-a-message tone he heard over and
over only the trumpeting call of elephants. The Mary
Beth Hudgins Doodlum Walker Mackenzie now bouncing gene of notions had struck Claudia Doodlum too,
her notions carrying her through a room of men in a
way that made them shift with their shirt collars suddenly too tight and an itch to flare nostrils in a scent
of some sort, irritating a nervous urge to either murder
or make love, and in Claudia's case maybe both. When
Powell first met her at a roadside bar, in his That Man
days, he looked from Claudia to Lisa Lee back to Claudia again, instantly thinking, Jesus God, I got the wrong
one, until he began to see how her clothes barely con-
tained her, like her lips could barely contain her rippling
tongue as she talked in lower and lower growls about
anything slick, fast, or hard, Powell recognizing the ex-
citing little lethal dangers in Lisa Lee he loved full-
blown and free of rein in Claudia, out of control, Claudia, in Powell's That Man days, barging in on him and
Lisa Lee on the couch into it as far as shirtless, Claudia
begging wildly, Strip me naked and tie me up, strip me
naked and tie me up and make me watch something
horrible! and Powell and Lisa Lee, complying, strap-

ping her into a kitchen chair, sitting her in front of the television, switching it to "History of the Harmonica Part 4 of 6" on Public Broadcast. Even then Claudia moaned and struggled with her bonds, complaining when they would come loose. Powell left a message to come home after the final elephant blast, hanging up, remembering suddenly an old hurt in Lisa Lee's voice saying one time Claudia had always been Bill Doodlum's favorite.

In the den, Doc had Louise Doodlum in a headlock on the couch and Lisa Lee was turning his bag out on its side, digging under Doc's directions. Louise had suddenly begun to pull everything out of the den closet and was flinging it across the room, some of Bill's books, a Panama hat, a box of family photographs. Louise took down a balsa-wood clipper model Bill had started and never finished and hammered her heel through it until the hull was flattened, crying, Lisa Lee letting her until Doc said, Enough is enough, Louise, and opened his bag for a shot. This isn't exactly what I had in mind but it will do, Doc said, slipping the needle into Louise Doodlum's arm that began to relax and turn fleshy again. This will make you tell us all your secrets, Doc said, noticing his watch and making a motion for Lisa Lee to turn on the color television in the corner. Yes, Louise, said Doc, straightening her legs on the sofa, you'll be telling us everything you know, every little Doodlum-hearted secret. A green and red smear in the middle of the television screen opened like a flower into a Christmas show winding up in song. Powell and Lisa Lee gathered up the closet-thrown things and settled Louise Doodlum in on the sofa with blankets and a pillow. I'm floating in the clouds, she informed them all.

What I want to know, said Doc, settling himself into Bill Doodlum's La-Z-Boy recliner and coaxing out the television remote from a stack of *Reader's Digest*s, is why you, Louise, gave our Sweet William the whole load of the pistol. Christ, Louise, he said, any one would have done it.

Louise seemed to push and roll beneath the blankets as if she felt she was some heavy object floating slightly submerged in a just-disturbed tub of water. Well, she said faintly, the first one was for love. Then, as if she was reciting the first ingredient in a recipe for something sweet to eat, she said again, The first one was for love, and the other eight were for something Bill said to me over dinner in front of company in nineteen sixty-six. Louise Doodlum's laugh was a slowly pumping hiss of air, finally inaudible beneath the blanket she pulled over her head.

Good night, Louise, said Doc, turning up the volume on the television with the remote.

Merry Christmas to you all, said Perry Como.

I feel so wonderfully wicked, said the blanket on the couch, its form gently heaving.

What Powell would stand wanting with Lisa Lee later

94

at the left-open broken place for the laying in of Bill Doodlum, was for her to slip the pistol beneath the starched, cedar-smelling folds of clothes in her chest of hopes, but Lisa Lee held her fingers to his lips for a silence, as if waiting for some sonic explosion of something that had just passed without sound overhead, Lisa Lee seeming to know that words are just sounds and that the sounds of love always follow where love has been.

GENIUS

GENIUS THINKS HIS BIG BELLY fits Carol's lumbar
the way the Gulf Stream runs hot and close up the back
spinal curve of the Carolina coast. Genius thinks Carol
is the hot semitropics and he is the jislike filament of
sun-broiled current running snug inshore. Genius pre-
tends the air in his lungs is the southeast trades that
blow the Gulf Stream in to the beach, turning water toe-
clear neck-deep. Genius likes to dog-paddle past the
clear-breaking waves to where the bottlenose dolphins
play. Fish-drunk and curious, the dolphins slap happy
against Genius' big belly before arcing out to sea in the
Stream.

Genius is waking fat and happy until he kicks off the

top sheet and sees it's not Carol the semitropics. Instead of Carol the semitropics he has Barbara the front-desk clerk. Genius can't think beyond mud flats at low tide when he looks at Barbara from the front desk. Genius goes out on the balcony of his room in the motel where Barbara works and hands his big belly up on the balcony railing. The real Gulf Stream looks like cut gray ribbon out past the breakers and Genius is downspirited. I have deceived myself again in my sleep, says Genius to himself. It downspirits me to think I am not the Gulf Stream. Genius holds his big belly in both hands and squeezes it like he wants to shoot something out of his belly button. A big belly takes energy away from even being flotsam today, he thinks. Genius goes back into his motel room to consider mud flats at low tide.

The last time Genius saw any part of Carol was when her fist came rushing up to his right eye and didn't stop and came right on coming. Genius saw part of her pretty pastel Easter skirt as he flipped over the railing on his way to the sidewalk, but Genius doesn't think that counts. It was Easter and they had been to the Easter parade. Carol had on her new pretty pastel skirt and the round straw Easter bonnet Genius had driven all the way to Williamsburg to get. The round straw Easter hat had a blue silk sash that matched Carol's eyes. After

Carol had punched Genius out and he sat leaning against the gutter curb feeling skin puff out from his cheek, Genius saw the round straw Easter hat with the sash that matched Carol's eyes sail over his head like a Frisbee. It sailed over his head and out into the street where it got run over flat by a car full of people who had come to see the Easter parade and were now going home.

The lifeguard on the beach is waving a red flag that matches his red lifeguard swim trunks. He is waving the flag and blowing a whistle for Genius to come in from so far out. Genius is floating on his back out past the breakers, out even farther than the good swimmers go. Genius floats and watches the lifeguard wave the red flag from his lifeguard stand. Sometimes Genius has to wait until the gentle swells turn him just right so he can see the lifeguard because sometimes Genius' big belly gets in the way. If Genius works his hands like flippers back and forth it looks like the lifeguard is moving back and forth behind a big hairy hill. If Genius relaxes his head deeper into the water the sun blinds his eyes and the water fills his ears so he can't see the lifeguard waving the red flag that matches his trunks or hear the whistle the lifeguard is blowing. He won't come out after me, thinks Genius. I have lived on the beach a very long time.

. . . . . .

Here is a list of things Carol has thrown at Genius: a sneaker with a toe full of sand in it, a coffee cup with a crescent of coffee in it, a raisin box with a half a box of raisins in it, and a picture of Genius holding a young girl under red and green plastic lanterns strung beside a pool. All of the things Carol has thrown at Genius have hit him in the face. The picture of Genius holding the young girl beside the pool Carol had to throw at Genius' face over and over because Genius was asleep. While Genius was asleep was always when Carol looked through his stuff and read his mail. When she found the picture of Genius holding the young girl she had to throw it as hard as she could on Genius' face over and over again until Genius finally woke up.

The southeast trades are blowing the Gulf Stream in and Genius has a bat kite hung up in the high-voltage wires by the motel. Genius is jerking on the bat kite string walking up close then backing back away. Barbara from the front desk has said to let her buy him a drink and forget the kite. Some surf nazis have skateboarded up and are making loud zap and sizzle sounds with their teeth and tongues. A police cruiser slows by, sees it's just Genius, and then speeds up to run over a cat. Genius pulls on the string to the bat kite hung up in the high-voltage wires until the string breaks and white-ribbons itself over a row of tourist cars parked in the motel parking lot. Genius winds in the string over the cars that the surf nazis check for dashboard change. From the bar in the motel Genius drinks a drink and watches the Gulf Stream blow in on the southeast trades.

Carol has said over the telephone there is no chance. Carol has said over the motel telephone there is no chance so much that the motel telephone bill is more than the motel room bill. Barbara at the front desk reads tourist people's postcards that tourist people send and listens in to Carol saying there is no chance to Genius over and over again. Once when she was listening in she heard Genius say he was going to shoot himself, and then there was a loud bang just as some surf nazis came into the lobby to steal matches and put boogers in the breath mint plate. Barbara from the front desk took out the master key and flung open the door to Genius' motel room. Genius was standing big-bellied naked by the telephone table, studying the heel of a shoe he was holding. The way he stood by the coiled-up cord, studying the heel, made Barbara from the front desk think at first the coiled cord was a snake Genius had just hammered with the shoe in the head and that maybe Genius was studying where he had gotten some snake head on the heel. When Barbara went back down to the front desk to listen in, Carol had already hung up and

100

the surf nazis had cleaned out the petty cash drawer and were gone and so was her purse. When the switchboard rang it was Genius who asked her to go to Ocean Eddie's seafood buffet and she went.

The girl Genius held under the green and red plastic lanterns is coming down to the beach. She says she has made the national swimming finals and she is coming down to practice and to see Genius. Genius thinks he is too fat for her now. His belly has swollen out drinking beer at the motel bar watching the Gulf Stream blow in and out on the southeast trades. Genius thinks when she sees him she will be disappointed. Genius thinks the lifeguard will get her if he is not careful. Genius is mad that she is coming down because she is too pretty for him and he is certain the lifeguard will get her. I'm coming down to the beach to practice and to see you because I like you says the girl Genius held under the green and red plastic lanterns. Genius is mad hanging up the telephone and Barbara the front desk clerk is unplugging her headset from listening in and she is mad too.

Carol and the reason there is no chance come down to the beach. The reason there is no chance drives a heavy-duty pickup truck with extra suspension. The doors on the heavy-duty pickup say Mr. Tire. In the back of the truck are brand new tires and retreads chained around canisters of compressed air. Carol and this reason there is no chance go out to Jungle Acres Putt-Putt and Genius hides behind the black plaster gorilla near the twelfth hole. Genius wants to page Mr. Tire over the intercom that is playing rock and roll. He wants to page Mr. Tire away from where Carol is bent over a short adult putter. If he can get Mr. Tire paged away he wants to break through the transplanted tropical reeds dying in the semitropics at Jungle Acres and say Mrs. Tire, I presume. Then Genius will fend off Mr. Tire with the short adult Jungle Acres putter. But Mr. Tire putts holes-in-one on the front nine and birdies the tenth so Genius gender checks the black plaster gorilla he's hunkered by and decides to go home.

The girl Genius held under the green and red plastic lanterns comes to the beach and shucks her clothes in Genius' motel room. In her bag are eleven bathing suits. Genius watches her swim from the boardwalk. He can hardly keep up walking along the boardwalk with her swimming in the surf against the current. She breaks splits in the rip curls and shimmers through faces of breakers. The lifeguards wave red flags that match their swim trunks and blow their whistles but they see they could never catch her. Her feet are long because she is tall and her long feet slap the water when she turns like the tail of a bottlenose dolphin. When she wades out and drips water over Genius' big belly she is not even winded. I felt the water go clean and warm just past the breakers, she says. There were big shapes moving deep under me but I wasn't afraid. The Gulf Stream, thinks Genius.

By dawn Genius has crept out of his room, leaving the young girl sleeping. Barbara at the front desk is face down in a pizza take-out box. Out in the parking lot Genius watches the offshore winds push cloud cover up over Arctic Avenue and the bat kite spins and dives side to side in horrible motions from the high-voltage wire it's tethered to. The bat kite's wings are ragged and its skeleton is bent but its flight is furious in the gusts that are pushing everything out to sea. The lifeguard stands stand empty, facing the waves coming in on the tide that seem hesitant about their break and collapse onshore. Genius strips down to his big belly and wades in the cold surf, cold because the wind has pushed the top of the water out to sea and stirred the deep cold bathos out of its cold black to break the breakers instead. Genius wades in and flipper fins his hands and feet out past the breakers until he is blown along with the foam seaward and then arches his spine so his big belly bulges out of the water and a motel guest from shore with binoculars would see what looked like a white-domed man-o-war way out or a child's beach ball deflating and ocean going. Genius thinks it isn't as pleasant as he thought but he knows how the Gulf Stream runs hot and clean just beyond the black swells he's pushing through so he relaxes and arches his back with his eyes open watching the pushed-up cloud cover cover the bluing black in the west, where below the drop in the west the beaches, the boardwalk, and the motels that border the boardwalk are now not lost behind one or two swells but lost for good, even when the canyons rush the big-bellied flotsam up to the peaks and down the canyon walls somewhere beyond even what he can see as bigger than his big belly, the big black swells of it all.

FISHBOY

I BEGAN AS A BOY, as a human-being boy, a boy with a secret at sea and sentenced to cook in Big Miss Magine's stone-scoured pot, my long fish body laid, tail flipping, into that solid stone pot, scales ripped and skin slipping from my meat tissue-threaded in the simmer, my body floating from my long, fish-bodied bones, my bones boiled through and through down to a hot bubbly sweet steaming broth, lisping whispers of steam twisting to the ceiling, curling in your curtains, speaking to you in your sleep.

I began as a boy with a whistling lisp and the silken-tipped fingers of another class. A boy with put-away memories of bedclothes bound tight about the head being knocked with a hammered fist; the smell of cigar and shoe leather, a slipping, gripped throw from a car into a side-road swamp. A given birthright there of a swimming, slithering beginning of life, holding water back to breathe through sour mudded filth and green surface slime. Put-away memories of pushed back bloody gums gnawing slugroot, the ripped frog muscle spasms tickling my tongue and the all-night chorus of croaking reproach; the bitter-centered snake eggs washed down with the stagnant sulphured water, all of it back up again splashing around my ankles, sunk in mire, new creations of life, wiggling and squirming, spasmed, web-footed, and scaled, and tiny dead reptilian eyes like pretty black beads in pearl. Sleeping for warmth in winter with wild dogs and precious suckled bitch's milk in exchange for an ear ripped with hair for the puppies to chew; sleeping with snakes for summer cool and puncture bites that clear infected eyes and sharpened my hearing to hear the sneeze of a rat to catch as a toy for this boy I began as, with still through it all the prissy wrist, the toe-pinched walk, a boy, who, had he any sisters, Big Miss Magine said, should have worn their handed-down dresses. This was me as that boy, to turn to fish when he went to sea, waiting the length of his short life in his cartonated box, waiting for the one boat to come in to the place where hardly any boats come.

Some boat.

Any boat.

A boat to brave itself through where the sea dunes and the sand waves folded over, no channel in and no channel out, a boy at the ready with his butter-turned knife to slice meats like fists from shells like plates.

That boy.

I had always been that boy in the cartonated box, waiting for the purple bus to pass through the places my whistling lisp would not let me speak, places I can whisper to you now with the ease of escaping steam, dark continent-calling places, places misplaced, name places like nothing in this language you and I share, places edging the round cratered lake where something large struck a long time ago, places along where the blacktop sinks through soft-bottomed bogs and erupts up the other side, a serpentine plumbing of the earth's thin surface, the purple bus leaning over bubbling quicksand corners, pushing with sand-spinning wheels and water-washed pipes, its white-eyed driver blind and dreaming them along the road he drove, steering the bus to where I always slept in wait.

And always I slept in my cartonated box listening in the early morning chill for the tottering of the bus into the rutted fishhouse lot, the sprung springs and ratching bad brakes, faces and elbows stuffing against the side windows as women reached beneath the seats for old jars of cold fish stew and grease-streaked brown bags of fried pork or some night animal snared on a porch

or caught in a closet, and I would wait in my box with
my thumbs tucked under my chin for Big Miss Magine
to unburden from the bus's breaking back, wait for her
to slip her lips like a big brown frog through the hole
in the box I watched the moon at night, and I would
watch, no matter the season's turn, how the blowing
slow of her big black breath would blue into a settling
spread of fog, her words, before laying her eye like a
painted egg against the moon-cut hole looking in to me,
the human-being boy, her, her words saying, *You is
mine, Fishboy, you is all mine.*

And then I would be the Fishboy, fetching in with
the other ones of those who came along on the big purple
bus from around the cratered lake, the lake an hour
across and a minute deep, with, in its middle, a speck
of heaven fallen so heavily it sent a wave against the
tide, the metal in its middle drawing steel and iron so
a spoon set on a table slides off across the floor and
swims a spooning spin through the peat-soaked water
down to what draws it; me fetching in with these that
live around the lake with crude tattoos and coiled mazes
cut into their faces with the talons and sharpened quills
of owl and osprey, nothing in their houses but clothing,
cloth, wooden stools, stone bowls, and kettles; me
fetching in to haul over the forty-weight baskets of red-
gilled brown fish with blue eyes and bottom-dwelling
shellfish like plates and platters, dumping them for the
big black women to slice out fillets with thin-bladed

knives with just enough curve, like a bent stiff prick, to work out the flesh of fish with a plunge and slicing of meats left limp, leaving the cutting out of the hard, pink-shelled shellfish to a red-rimmed drunk, a soft-skulled child, and me, the human-being boy, the Fishboy, Fishboy running between filling baskets of fish and shellcut in my tied-around-the-neck plastic fronted apron, slipping on the gut-spilt floor, watching the little flat-bottomed skiffs pack out with a basket strung from a boom and wondering would a big boat ever come, would a big boat ever come with room for me; and when one would come, it would be me begging pardon for a chance to wade down into waist-deep icy black bilge water in the hold, unloading the trash and swimming in the filth to unstopper the draincocks of fishheads and rotten stock so the storage bins could drain dry, washing dark 'tween deck bins with a rag on a stick, stacking in the boards for more of the fifteen tons of sparkling sharp ice I would shovel, bloody knuckling the crystals pink, praying out loud, *Please Captain, please Mate, see, it's me, the Fishboy! See, look here, clean there, and stacked right, fore and aft! Please, see, see how I've worked, see how I'll work until I choke on the frozen smoke* . . . and then, but always I would hear the holler, *More fish! More shellcut!* Fishboy! Then up the hold ladder while the hatches clatter down, and then not the Captain, not the Mate, not a winchman, nor even the cook but the lowliest seaman whose work I'd saved and

109

done in the hold as my own would come out of some down-corner bunk or from around a corner of a hose shack, eye glazed and trouser stained and say, *Get along there, Fishboy, this is union scripts, my lovely, get off now, you, no papers, no work!* and I would be lifted up from the deck by the side of his hard-swung boot and I would sail hearing his rotten rodent-tooth laugh, *Thanks for the help in the hold!* and I would slap the cold wet concrete apron of the pack-out pier next to the stacked-up baskets of fish and shellcut, doubly full now for me to catch up, for me to carry straining and slipping across the cutting-room floor, watching out the open side of the shed the union scripts casting off, and I would turn not to look, hoping anyone seeing the wet on my face would think it only the scales thrown by the fishes' flipping tails, emptying the baskets along the table deeper into the cutting shed darkness until the last fish would slide beneath the upheld fillet knife of Big Miss Magine, pointing at me, saying in the low black-breath whisper, almost in fog, *You is mine, Fishboy—you is all mine.*

Soda Time!
Fish*boy*!
Lunch bags and glass jars come out with the big black women drying in the cold sun on the broken-down dock, perched on pilings like feathering blackbirds, speaking that around-the-cratered-lake gobble talk and paying

me a nickel to dive down into the fillet-gutted waste
water that sluices through the cutting shed, emptying
out into the creek, paying me a nickel to go down to
where the soda machine lies at the bottom, fallen
through its place on the dock and still plugged in un-
derwater. *Get me a cold soda, Fishboy, a red one!* and
holding my breath for as long as it took I could, I could
even hold it long enough to steal a cold soda for myself
and sit on the bottom of the gut-watered creek, watching tiny fish feed in the clouds of waste that bloomed
overhead in the water while I drank.

These were the long days in the short length of my
life as the Fishboy, the sun slipping into the cratered
lake like a figure eight of flame. I would make the last
go-around call for fish to fillet and shell to cut, letting
the big black women have their pick of the rotting fish
left from the bottom of the union scripts or local boats,
letting them take the souring fish with the milky ruined
blood home, wrapped in their front-tied plastic aprons,
the women drunk on finishing the last work of the day
and laughing at my whistling lisp, singing, *Finish fish!*
Finish fish! Take home your finish fish! And I would
shuffle dead tired through the sand with my own finish
fish, usually just the head of some dull-eyed carcass I'd
simmer into stew over a driftwood fire beside my cartonated box, shuffling with it tucked in my apron in my
pinched-toed walk, not looking at where the purple
bus's back would bend beneath the flat worn-footed

111

weight of the big black women, and I would wait until the white-eyed driver at the wheel would fall asleep to dream them home, wait until I was sure the bus was gone before I would peek out my moon-cut hole, but the bus would roll quietly over the dusted-up sand, never as far as I thought, and no matter how long I waited, waited until I thought it was safe to press my eyeball to the moon-cut hole, I would always see one seeing back, in the corner of the bus's back window, the bus leaving the lot on its way around the cratered lake, always a red-blue-purple-painted egg of an un-blinking eyeball staring straight back into my own.

THE THEORY OF MAN

I LOOK FOR ME and my best ex-friend Charles in the pages of the morning paper. I peel and spread the print, peel and spread the print that the sun over my shoulder yellows. Everything is about the heat. I read to Charles about the man who was fishing for smallmouth bass and landed a pair of sand sharks instead. Charles digs around in his newly stolen toolbox and says, Bullshit and I say, True fact, it's in Tommy's Tidewater Tacklebox. A marine scientist says the freshwaters are thinning, the sea creeping brackish. I peel and spread through Metro. Another altercation at the courthouse, city fathers fistfight over rules of order, police report gunplay over parking places. There's an artsy photo of our empty reservoir, a bunch of hundred acres of jig-sawed cratered clay. A five-hundred-dollar fine for watering your lawn, the mayor earns two while hydrants are wrenched open and dry. On the front page a fuzzy photo of the deer that stumbled into town to lick plate glass. The editorial fear is of fire.

I still don't see us, I say to Charles. Charles says, Check comics and classifieds.

Behind full-page auction bid ads for businesses on the skids are the news-filler pages with items of no conclusion or consequence. I see the police are still shaking their heads over the double murder-suicide in Charles' and my neighborhood. We were definitely out of town for that one. Paper says they had to use jackhammers to open cemetery topsoil. There was funereal heat-stroke at the service even though everyone knows the Baptists have the best AC in town. You drive by their Sunday-sermon marquee and it remains the same, it says to Please Pray for Rain.

Charles is attempting torque shoulder-deep in the air-craft engine when the ratchet designed for high-per-formance Italian sports cars slips its grip on our Mr. Goodwrench sparkplug. Charles withdraws his blood-creased knuckles and with all his might flings the wrench up on the roof of an old abandoned hangar. From out of the hangar comes a coo and flutter of pigeon reposition but nothing ever feathered flies.

Here we are below Obits, I say, beneath the survivors' lists of our town's most recent departees, the terminally coughed, the unwakeably napped, the head-on windshield-sculpted.

Read us, says Charles. Charles wraps his metrically split fingers in the front of his shirt.

I read us to Charles. I read us under Beach Blaze Termed Non-Suspicious. It says the investigators of the early morning fire that completely destroyed the Sportsman Inn failed to find any evidence of arson, and that Fire Chief Willie Warren stated spontaneous combustion is not all that uncommon in unseasonable heat such as we are experiencing.

Charles says he shares two theories of unexplained fires with Willie Warren, sponny combo being his second favorite. Read on, he says.

I read on about how Chief Warren says it could have been started in the basement by old paint cans and rags left lying around in all this heat, or he says it could have been started by—Guess what, I say to Charles and Charles asks with hope, Rats chewing matches? and I say, That's right, that's the chief's second theory. Rats chewing matches has always been Charles' favorite.

Charles smiles and turns to let his face fill with sun. His open eyes have that soft-focus glaze I recognize as further theory formulation. This morning he has been working on a corollary to his secondary theory of this summer's heat. Charles says the planet has entered an orbit too near the sun. He says, Have you noticed how the sun doesn't rise like an orange ball any more? He says it is more like a curtain of *flame* lifting on the horizons around us. As usual, Charles' theory is tainted with truth. At nine o'clock already the sidewalk concrete sizzles your spit.

I pass my hand as shadow in front of Charles' face and Charles resumes his adjustments. He says some of the gauges aren't working, exactly, do I mind? I say, No, let's go, we're going to be late. I fold up the newspaper to show us to Our Boss the Crackpot as Charles drops the cowling and kicks away the chocks from the wheels. We bounce through the grassy parking square motoring onto the runway. Gas is sloshing in the tanks we could not afford to fill. Which ones? I ask Charles as he opens the throttle and lets off the brakes. The runway begins to rush beneath us, the trees at the end float trunkless in the mirror of their own mirage. Charles says, Which ones what? and I say, Which ones aren't exactly working? Charles burns his nose underbiting a cigarette as he pulls the wheel to his chest. We lift to climb pre-treely and I count pine needles brushing past. Nothing works *exactly*, he says.

My forward view of the earth is dimmed by a splatter of wind-driven drivelets of oil across my side of the front-canopy glass. I point this out to Charles who notes that there are certainly none on *his* side. I turn in my seat to stare through the glass in my door.

The ocean is a haze of evaporation. In our harbor

ships are held by thread against tips of rail along the shore. They wait for the trains that come down from mountains dead with coal. The fingered spread of switchyard rail reaches for the ocean like it is an oasis. These are the tracks that spear the heart of our neighborhood, Charles' and mine and all our neighborly neighbors. In our neighborhood the tracks are littered with pieces of coal the size of dice flung from the rumble of the two-oh-eight, the six-fourteen or the eleven-fifty-seven Midnight Howl. In winter sometimes one of our neighbors' children is caught on the tracks in the early dark December brings. Sometimes a neighborhood child will apparently become engrossed in a trackside splatter of slop tossed from a conductor's dinner or become busy savoring the last puff on the butt of a soggy cigar spit from the window of a passing caboose. In the kind of neighborhood we live in if the engineer is ever aware that he has struck something on the tracks he'll look along there next time through for cattle hooves or children's shoes before checking his watch and reaching above his head for the whistle cord to signal his arrival home.

Charles knows to follow the tracks west, a black and steel stitchery straight through cut-over forest and parched earth, the crop failures similar shades of old brown paste. I think about finishing the newspaper but I am succumbing to the rapture of flight. The coastal plain slips beneath the green rumpled roll of the pine-skinned piedmont. Drunk on the obscurity that altitude affords, my eyelids become heavy as I contemplate a landscape as interesting as Astroturf carpet.

Charles shakes me awake so I think we are near where we are supposed to be going so I touch Charles' hands on the wheel. The nose lowers. Trees begin to limb and houses window. I see that we are still far short of the mountains. Charles has spotted a coal train full-throttled for our neighborhood and the switchyard ships beyond. Once again I will be made to endure one of Charles' displays of aggression toward trains for which I am partially responsible. Our gentle descent breaks into a strut-screaming kamikaze plunge, a wing-wobbling strafe out of the sky-spread sun. The geometry of sound that our intersection with the train makes scatters wildlife and livestock alike. We climb for altitude to dive again on the train from behind. Charles checks us back above the lead engine and in a clearing ahead we dip alongside. The engineer gives us the finger with both hands in gloves firemen wear to protect their wrists from sparks. I obediently take the wheel at powerline level while Charles unbuckles his pants and presses his pimpled rear end against his side of the canopy glass. Charles has everything between his legs squeezed behind him, presenting the engineer with what Charles calls a Flying Fruit Salad. The engineer now shakes a walkie-talkie at us. Tora tora tora, locomotive FUCK, says Charles as he settles in his seat and lifts us up into the sun.

It goes to this. I have known Charles all his life. There were never any symptoms of aviation in his family. No crop dusters, no barn stormers, no ace pilot heroes. Our heroes rode horses and slaughtered their enemies who were easy to find in fields and forests and floating in off the seas. Our heroes never had to look up to seek out and slay any extra.

Charles says his interest in flying began the morning he woke up in the cabin of a small plane heading high out over the Atlantic without a pilot. This was during the beginning of Charles' wild years, when Charles would disappear for days with real estate people up to Atlantic City or to some hunting lodge on the Eastern Shore. I was never invited along although I knew some of the real estate people through when they would call me up to paint a house that niggers had lived in and they wanted to sell it with Colonial colors to white people, the Williamsburg blue, the Duke of Gloucester cream. They would call me up to roll white people paint over the purple passion walls in the bedroom and please for God's sake take down those squares of mirrors off the ceiling over where the bed used to be.

So Charles says one morning he sort of came to remembering he was on a private plane to somewhere some broker was flying himself to, but the broker had passed out during a midflight fantasy in the back with one of the party girls. The automatic pilot had overflown the landing field a few hours earlier, its alarm beeping having finally woken Charles up. Charles says he sat in the empty pilot's seat and studied all the dials and gauges and levers and pedals and buttons and after about fifteen minutes decided he could take the auto pilot off, him figuring the switch to do that with as being a black lever like a match stick near where you turn numbers on a dial to set the computer-compassed course. So Charles put his feet on the pedals he knew controlled the rudder, wrapped a hand around the wheel, and with the other flicked the auto pilot off.

Charles, on wings, dipped the plane and then lifted the nose, what he says is the natural inclination among novice pilots, to lift the nose, and that is what Charles did until the plane was swallowed up in a rolling cloud of cumulus. Charles says he noticed the charms on the ignition key ring were hanging at an odd angle and his head lightened. Then some little red lights shone brightly and the engine noise slid up and down the octave scale, and then, as he pushed and turned the wheel, the key ring charms went spread flat on the flight panel like bedside table change. The broker and the party girl bundled in a roll against the back of Charles' seat and the girl screamed as the broker pushed her off. Charles said the feeling of plummet was oddly satisfying, like as a kid him coasting his bicycle down Jackson Hill Road at night towards the main intersection in

120

town, and he would close his eyes and take his hands off the handlebars, giddy with broken boredom as he became a willing hostage to momentum, gravity, gyroscopics, and the chancy prospect of sudden impact. Charles said in that pure moment when the plane ripped out of the bottom of the cloud and earth eased up from below he developed one of his first theories. He said that fear is only in the implication of science, that death is only in its application. After that incident Charles had a twelve-week subscription of the *Christian Science Monitor* sent to our house but after Charles wrote Pray for Payment over the second and third invoices and mailed them back the newspaper stopped appearing in rolled tight little bundles like batons that were handy for hurtling at garbage-tipping dogs that strayed into our yard.

Charles moved out of our neighborhood in the second season of his wild years and I didn't see him much. He was living in unsold condos that his real estate friends built. When they sold the one he was living in he would just move into another. He had taken up flying and said it was going great. He would call me up from the airport on Friday evenings to tell me where he was flying some real estate people to and tell me the hours he was accumulating. From what I got over the phone Charles was a client softener. He had real estate credit cards for restaurants and bars and free tickets and cars and all the blow you could blow. Once when I was low bid on the interior trim for Sandpiper Keys Condos Charles brought some clients around where I was on my hands and knees with a detail brush and Charles walked them through to the deck around the kitchen and up the back to bypass me where I was working. On Friday evenings after a while the phone would ring and I would be outside, drinking a beer on the porch, picking paint from underneath my nails with a pocketknife, waiting for the six-fourteen to roll past, and I would let the phone ring and ring, not answering, and after a while the phone calls on Friday began to stop coming altogether.

I had a feeling I would see Charles again when his real estate friends built so many condos and projects that there weren't enough people with that kind of money to buy them. Not in our town or the next few out in the radial spread. My own business was falling off. I was getting by on a little renovation, termite damage, and an out-of-town out-of-control car off Beekman's Curve that made a drive-through out of this lady's dining room and den. I had heard Charles was out of the real estate business and into the blow clientele of teeth-gnashing snot-nosers with heart palpitations. You would see his car out in front of the Rendezvous Lounge which everybody knew was being watched by the two undercover feds in the schoolyard across the street playing catch with a couple of mitts and a tennis ball.

I began to see Charles again after the evening he called me up to come over and see the Magic Show. I

went over to the room he had rented at Big Bill's Beach
Cabanas and Charles met me at the door with a revolver
to my throat until he threw the bolts on the lock and
then spent five minutes folding back the edge of the
drapes asking me was I followed. He had this real blow-
bitchy, snow bunny type with him then, plastic high
heels and a three-day dress. For the Magic Show
Charles dumped a Zip-Lock bag of powder into a mixing
bowl and then spooned chalky white baby laxative into
it saying Abracadabra . . . two ounces into . . . FOUR
ounces! Through this substance excess our transfor-
mations into the anti-us were truly magical, almost bib-
lical in their purity. The anti-me, the anti-Charles, the
anti–Snow Bunny Bitch.

The anti-Charles went out and scurried the perimeter
of Big Bill's Beach Cabana, a pistol-packing rat in a
crease of wall and floor. I listened in spellbound fas-
cination at the unfolding account of the anti–Snow
Bunny Bitch's life in words of one syllable, the fast-food
fry cook with aspirations dentally hygienic. The anti-I
searched her sentence fragments for an opening among
the most common flossing mistakes so that the anti-I
could tell her my own story, the frustrated portrait artist
trapped in a world of low-bid trim and latex, but her
points on popcorn trapped in the rear molars were so
perceptive I could only sigh, longing to draw her near
and smell her sour breath and fish-fried hair, longing

123

to kiss her filthy neck and shiny ears just to taste the bitter unwashed wax within. How wonderful the magic!

Soon after, during his fifteen-thousand-dollar blow crisis, Charles, and this, his girl Hazel, came to live with me in my trackside Dutch oven hovel. Hazel said she had never actually lived in hell before but I betted her that she had visited often. I told her I hoped she would not be put off by my neighbors who are niggers or by my scab-blackened front yard. What happens is, sparks shower from the wheels of coal trains braking their descent from the coastal plain into our port city. Sometimes small, well-formed flames carpet the railway, igniting the coal dust and the dice-sized chunks of coal my neighbors don't collect in summer. Sometimes these well-formed flames sneak out of the ditches and march across my front yard, combusting everything in their path, including the garbage-tipping stray dog Lincoln Logs of fossilized shit, and then I have to get up off the porch where I have been watching all this drinking beer and wave pee across their sorry little columns to turn their advance. I said again I hoped she would not be put off by all of this and she and Charles took their bags and went into the house.

That was in the hot spring of this long hot summer though it feels a hundred years ago, before the fifteen-thousand-dollar debt crippled Charles' mind and before what I did to him next. Charles was still of the mind to formulate theories. His primary theory of the blistering summer heat was that, like all adult stars its age, our sun was toying with total collapse. Although its plumes seemed to surround us, that was only so it could get one last look at its only worthwhile creation in this insignificant solar system. Otherwise, said Charles, if you look directly into the sun every day like I do, you will notice that the core is growing almost imperceptibly smaller.

This has been one of those summers where no air moves. Hazel was miserable in the heat and miserable with the trains. You have to understand that when the coal trains come through you can feel their approach a couple miles off. Then the floors shake, soup in pots sloshes and tables vibrate across the floor with chairs dancing between their legs. Anything glass and touching in the cabinets above the sink will clink and sing like you have a flock of hopped-up songbirds in there eager for release.

What turned us all this summer was when Our Boss-to-be, The Crackpot, bought the Sportsman Inn to renovate and I was low exterior bid. Charles said he knew the guy in a funny, third-hand sort of way and told me to get my money up front. I got it in cash and with the outdoor work and pocket money by the middle of June I was beer bottle brown and drunk even asleep. I'd come home from work and Charles would be on the phone asking someone please not to have him killed for a lousy fifteen thousand dollars, goddamnit, and Hazel would be naked on the floor of their room in front of the box fan I bought them. I would take a beer out on the porch and watch my neighbors unscissor folding aluminum lawn chairs along the tracks, awaiting the arrival of the six-fourteen, waiting for it to cleave the heat and shed some breeze.

It was always my theory that Hazel was getting ready either to leave Charles or to lose her French-fried mind the night she came out and sat on the porch with me, t-shirt and panty shameless. She asked me why didn't I go up on the railroad shoulder and enjoy the six-fourteen arrival of weather with my neighbors and I told her I didn't want either to lessen their opinions or to live up to their expectations by falling down drunk into the ditch between where they sat and where we were. I told her I had just won low bid on the interiors of the rooms at the Sportsman Inn. The Crackpot had naturally picked out that blue-green southern seaside resort color for the rooms, a color you never see in nature except maybe when the sky is getting ready to drop down a waterspout that will come ashore and suck up all the tourists taking pictures of its approach with sun-lotion-smeared camera lenses. Some color paints I can paint all day and some honestly give me the creeps and I throw out the brushes and burn the drop cloths later.

Hazel said she had to do something, she had to get out of the house. I said would a paintbrush fit her hand and she turned both of hers palm up on her naked knees

126

and I took a shameless look at t-shirt and panty-contoured symmetry. Hazel asked did the rooms where we would work have AC and I said, Yes and TV too. Cabled color.

Charles did not seem to mind. Charles was trying to develop a theory of debt and as long as I paid Hazel a fair wage he could factor ex–Snow Bunny income into an equation of repayment.

I was also hoping having Hazel having income would allow Charles to subtract from his debt equation his going through my pockets when I passed out, wrecking my car, stealing my clothes and selling my paint. Charles was in bad shape and I took his formulation of debt theory as an encouragement that he was getting better, reading theory formulation as fever broken.

Hazel helped me paint the Sportsman Inn motel walls the Crackpot green for about fifteen minutes, or about the time it takes for motel AC to crank cool and tourist-proof TV to warm up. Hazel leaned on bunched up pillows across the bed, a patient recuperating from Magic Shows and coal trains and nigger neighborhood heat with eight to ten hours daily of game shows and soap operas. It was really okay all the same with me. Whenever my plaster bucket ran low on tallboy Budweisers and ice she never complained about running over to the 7-Eleven and getting more as long as it was during the midday newscasts or extended commercial breaks. This was well worth minimum wage to me.

127

Charles should have had a theory about all of this, about what would be inevitable about leaving alone together a man and a woman, day after day, in rooms with beds as central furniture, not even theorizing the tangentials of the man drinking and the woman bored, one day falling into the next like the numbers on the motel doors, doors that lock, day after day, man-woman-bed, man-woman-bed, man-woman-bed. Charles should have had a theory about all of this but apparently he did not.

At home in the evenings after Charles and Hazel would go to bed I could hear them through my Dutch oven hovel cardboard walls doing it, and Charles was even louder about it than Hazel. And sometimes Hazel was so loud that on afternoons when I knew the roofing contractors were at the Sportsman Inn working I would have to grab a pillow and stuff it over her face when things got crucial. But Charles would work himself into something sounding oriental, like he was delivering a karate chop to a stack of bricks. It didn't bother me all that much but in our neighborhood sometimes porch lights would come on and dogs would bark.

Discretion to Hazel meant waiting until Charles was asleep and the Midnight Howl would come rumbling through to cover our noise and then she would sneak into my room and then we would do it while the house shook and the cabinets chirped and the furniture danced and the roar of the engines would be followed by the clatter of the coal cars rolling over a crimp in the steel rail out by our house. You could be in bed and count the cars in clicks and clacks, and most trains had about two hundred, so I'd keep a rough count and hurry to finish with Hazel before we ran out of train, before the sudden hushed rush of the last car and caboose, and then Hazel would detour into the john and I would turn against the cardboard wall smelling my own beer breath and thinking of prayers I should say, falling asleep before I could pray them.

The catalyst of this us-equation is an old coal-burning engine painted maintenance yellow. It pulls about a dozen flat beds and boxcars. On the flat beds are cranes to rip old ties and lay new rails, and the boxcars are full of hand tools—a couple are fitted with bunkbeds and a galley for the roving crews. Coming down the tracks one night after eleven thirty this yellow engine approached just like the Midnight Howl, the same dirty rumble, the same blasts of signal at the Eastend crossing that are low and mournful. Hazel and I had just started when what we thought was the Midnight Howl on the tracks outside seemed to pass prematurely, the too-fast rush of the last car's hush, Hazel howling in the sudden silence, Charles standing in the door.

In a few minutes later, when the real Midnight Howl arrived, we three sat about the kitchen table as we held it in its place, our hands holding on its edges, a seance of the real Charles, the real Hazel, the real me, sitting beneath the bare-bulbed light as it swung from its cord casting random shadows on our faces wet with sweat and eyes unblinking, Charles' temples pulsing with every clipped clatter of the passing coal-car wheels, two hundred hoppers of furnace grade fuel thundering past, overloaded and ahead of schedule, click clack, click clack, click clack.

A couple of days after Hazel announced that she was reuniting with her husband, The Crackpot, I stood with everyone else watching the Sportsman Inn burn to the ground. Charles said a business associate of The Crackpot had told him the police take pictures of suspicious-fire-scene bystanders so Charles was not around. Charles had used one of my old paint cans to mix the sodium chloride, topped off by a rubber filled with sulphuric acid. The Sportsman Inn was a clean burn, the first coupon Charles would clip from his fifteen-thousand-dollar crisis-payment book.

I felt a sadness, watching the fire eat out the roof over the indoor sea-water pool. I had been low bid on the interior veneer. There was more exposed beam and cross brace in that place than a Lutheran church. The Crackpot suggested to Charles that he get the keys to the Inn from me, and I gave them to him. I felt a sadness about all of this. Maybe it is because I am a careful painter and I had been extra careful on the exterior trim and hadn't splattered hardly any paint at all. I don't know. Maybe it was just the sadness one feels in the beginning settlement of old familiar debts.

This day Charles and I have been summoned to conclude our repayment business at The Crackpot's mountaintop estate. I am hoping this is the end. I did not realize in the beginning how easily the debts between us are assumable. We have been purveyors of porno bimbos, we have carried satchels of cash up the coast and body bags out to sea. We have been skycaps to scum, the simple handlers of someone's thug luggage.

The morning paper proves us to be something new, we are the rats chewing matches, we are the all-this-heat. It has been a long fifteen-thousand-dollar summer and it is time for a break in the weather.

Charles comes in high over the estate and circles wide to see if there is anything municipal about these mountains. There is a water-tower town to the east and a mirage of airport that turns out to be a shopping center.

The Crackpot has forbidden us to land in his driveway any more. The last time we did we diverted a sedan of late-arriving guests into a stand of two-hundred-year-old boxwoods. Charles and I both had our feet on the brakes as the wheels screamed and our straining sheet-metal wing flaps buckled and popped like they were about to wrench off. We were running out of driveway and the old house was running up to meet us. The house is so old that because both the rear and front doors were open I could see completely through the place and I saw people crowding out the hallway to flee into the backyard beyond. Luckily our tires caught in the flowerbed brick dividers along the front walk and the only casualties were the red tulips, whose heads blew off in the wash of our propeller as Charles turned to taxi, and a couple of wind chimes and hanging plants on the front veranda became aerodynamic. Drapes in a front room ballooned inward as The Crackpot leaned out and glared as I waved to him hello.

This day there is a graded space for us behind the estate so Charles spirals over The Crackpot's barbecue to make our approach. We turn in tight circles over the parked cars, the long white tables of buffet, the barbecue poolside where last time Charles leg-wrestled a state senator and then punched out the son who needed it. We bank and glide and I see Hazel. I see Hazel in ground zero of our concentric descent. It must be her in a shiny gold dress, centered in a scattershot of hard dick. I had heard she was capitalizing on being fine, the prime rate agreeing with her. She is gold and shiny off the wing we are pivoting on, a sun-struck drip off a honey sandwich into a path of ants. As we flatten near the treetops I see it is her face, and her face is the first to look up while the men around her continue to look down, probably deep into her dress.

This day we are not guests, we are merely grocery clerks, errand boys, messengers maybe. We are not even off the plane, just taxiing, when Hazel herself appears with a small snakeskin valise. I unlatch my door and lean out to fold it open when in a pure grace-Hazel motion she presses in towards me as if to offer a kiss but instead deftly clasps with a ratchet sound the snakeskin case to my wrist with a handcuff. Her lips, formerly puckering to place a kiss, retract across her teeth, making words as she withdraws. Take this right back down to the beach, guard it with your lives, she says. You are done, she says. It's been real.

Charles ignores her, ignores me, ignores us. My face, which is still forward and not unready to accept her kiss, is slammed with canopy glass before I can even ask who at the beach will have the key to the cuffs.

Now Charles looks at me and brings the engine to life. We ascend. We climb higher in the coolness, dipping valleys and turning peaks until we find the rails where they lie below, spun on ledges peeled from rock, shiny with use and overbreak-shaded. Our roadmap home through the plain to where the beaches burn and our neighborhood awaits the arrival of the six-fourteen weather.

Charles says he smells something. He says he doesn't think it is his socks this time, let him smell the snakeskin valise. I hold it for him under his nose. Do you smell that? he asks. Charles says that sweaty leather smell is agitated nitroglycerine.

I start to jimmy the lock on the valise with one of

Charles' newly stolen tools but he says, Don't, it might be rigged. Then Charles has a theory. Charles believes our final payment is in the snakeskin and that the charge is atmospherically controlled, a barometered bomb that will blow with our descent onto the coastal plain. Charles is pretty calm about this so I ask him if he knows something that I don't know and he says he just has theories, that no one really *knows* anything.

I tell Charles I guess I could at least save him if I jumped out of the plane and Charles says, Yes, I suppose you could. Climb, I say and we do.

We linger in indecisive spirals over the opening of the piedmont plain, a buzzard on a thermal. Below us in a turn in the track as tight as a cripple's knees we see a string of black humped cars in a slow, side-binding descent. Charles relates a theory about the train below. He says the kinetic energy stored in the train at the mountain's peak would be enough to unwind it completely across the state, unassisted by its engines, which he says at this point are merely inhibitions of momentum.

Over our shoulders we turn to watch the train before we wing away homeward, load after load of the earth's dead heart mined into shiny black pieces, the car couplings clasped in worn fraternal grips.

FEAST OF THE EARTH,
RANSOM OF THE CLAY

WE BURY OUR DEAD in the muscle of our town, in the shouldered hillock of clay once an island in a river finished flowing. The rest of town rests around its heart on the low relief of the alluvial plain, the sandy loam long yielded to the weathering ages of wear. From a folding chair on top of Cemetery Ridge you can sort the soil strata by the tops of the trees below, their foliage betraying their roots—the evergreen against the seasonal, roots suitable for the sand or for the loam but not for the clay. Nothing grows well on Cemetery Ridge. Nothing we plant here is ever expected to bloom.

Behind this ridge they laid bare the clay for the spur line of the railroad. Beneath this raw overhang beside

135

the tracks runoff from summer storms has carved out ragged ditches and hollowed out some caves. If you are a schoolboy in our town, you may be tempted to hole up here in ambush of the evening freight with your slingshot and your can of rocks, and sometimes some shanty-weary mongrel bitch will come sniffing around, sniffing out some place to lie in and squeeze out her litter. But in our town Mr. Leon lives in these caves behind Cemetery Ridge. He lives here the best he can, slathering his beard and his bald head, licking his alluvial walls, sucking the mud where it is wet.

Of the twice we always expect to see Mr. Leon, the first is in the evenings when he slips from the face of the cliffs on his way to our neighborhoods. Mr. Leon roams. Sometimes a dog will bark at Mr. Leon's full-mudded appearance, a man a patchwork of crusty fractures in dried gray. Sometimes a child, seeing the city-park statue stepped from its pedestal and coming down the street at dusk, will cry. But our dogs do not bite unless you are a thief or plan to become one, and someone will always come out to hush a child, and Mr. Leon makes his way. Bark, you bastards, or, Cry, you little shits, is all that Mr. Leon will say, shaking his fist in that way that worn-out men will, pouring some kind of anointment into the air.

The other time we expect to see Mr. Leon is at the funerals of our dead—like today. In the middle of this cakebox spread of granite and marble atop Cemetery

Ridge we wait for the out-of-town late arrivals and the tick-tock walk of Mr. Leon. The sun is bright off the worn, standing-around suits, mail-ordered and living-room-tailored. And there are crisp glints of light in the hems of the dresses patched and passed around by the grocery bagful. There is no hurry on this side of the family. They have arrived early and will be the stragglers later along the alleyways of the marble-stoppered clay. While they wait, they break away weeds from around the low-humped inscribed rock, resettle the chipped glass baskets of plastic flowers, the paper pots of front yard blooms. Little words. News, regret, respect. Within reach, these people smooth one another's arms through the worn clothing, then their hands return to the white that is working in their fingers, the worried twists of tissue, the thick, cupped curls of the hand-rolled smoke. The men's chins are held higher today, bolstered by the unaccustomed thick knots of the shoe-wide neckties they wear. This allows these men a proudness they do not possess, a skin-straightening effect in their faces for a few instants against years in the sun. Some of the women seem to notice this subtle flush of youth restored to their husbands here at the end of a life, and such women work up a little sob just for themselves.

The other side of the family arrives in unfamiliar out-of-town cars, shiny. Dark windshields. Music in the last of the caravan that scatters gravel past the paupers' square up the cart path past where the Beales and the Chessons and the Lamberts and the Warrens are all laid out, and then, instantly, alarmingly, the newcomers park alongside the brass-railinged coffin of our most newly deceased.

Spiked heels and hand-stitched leather feel for footing, and there are belly thrustings from the long ride, starch crackling. Chatter from the last caravaned car in the back. Singsong handbag indecision. Is it the addiction of tobacco or the obligation of tissue? To hell with it, leave it in the car, it will all be over with shortly.

The son of the deceased adjusts his entourage into seats adjoining what he calls, over cocktails, his previous administration. There are some missed looks, some coat and shawl tucks, spit whispers and lip-read warnings, but hands manage to cross divides from both sides and there is a quiet conference with the man in black with the book, the noddings to begin it, let's begin, okay, Father?

Would that it were so simple in our town. Would that it were so simple to lay in this one old dead lady, to dismiss this bird-calling biddy who lived at the end of the road to Cemetery Ridge. The bird-calling biddy, flinging sometimes to her nearest neighbor, the cave-dwelling Mr. Leon, a nickel or a piece of pie wrapped in newspaper. The bird-calling biddy, night after night, year after year, that phonograph record on her hi-fi turned so far up, her late husband's world-famous Summerset Birdcalls of Enchantment. Night after night, year after year, the whole neighborhood, the warbling, the trilling, the long deep swooning and the high-pitched chirping. Night after night, louder with her age and the wear on the phonograph record, and her not turning it all the way up to better hear her husband's calls but to hear him draw his breath before them, like if you lived in our town before he died you could hear him do at every outdoor party with summer and gin, you could hear him draw his breath across the backyard barbecue over the sizzle of grease in the grill, over the rattle of ice in your glass, her husband drawing his breath before setting off over the Eastern Seaboard in search of mates, wooing them through the trees, purging the nests, warning the young. Would that it were so simple in our town to dismiss this old lady, the bird-calling biddy, quickly, the one who played that phonograph record over and over so loud that it was something that you ceased to hear until it stopped and we knew that she was dead, the needles so grooved into the worn-out vinyl you heard just a long raw rumble punctuated by squeaks, birds drowning in the surf of an ocean, the nighttime soundtrack for our landlocked streets.

Our quiet streets, her vacant house, this new funeral for our dead—and, of course, Mr. Leon.

Just as we waited for the late arrivals from out of town we wait for Mr. Leon, because this evening the questions from the absent bedridden and from the indisposed will not be about you and how you dressed and how you fared. The whispers will be Did Mr. Leon show up?

He did?

Did he . . . do anything?

Did he . . . *eat* anything?

A straggler appears on the opposing hill, canebrake stick raised in our direction not so much in greeting as in some self-directed indication of further forward progress. This is a setback for the out-of-towners, those with the two-hour drive and the afternoon appointments. They settle back in impatient folding-chair slumps. A southeast breeze is all that is commencing. It brings up pine scent from the sand-floored forest. The soil spaded at our feet smells sweet, its sugar attracting dime-sized shadows of woods spiders working their ways to the edge of the chiseled clay.

Mr. Leon spits a large wad of something among the paupers' places and sets off toward us, leaning heavily in a sideboard motion on his stick. He poles himself downstream the cart path afloat atop his shoes. From the folding chairs, those who know know that Mr. Leon is wearing his finest—the homemade vest of domestic cat, tails adrip down the front, the head of a tom on each shoulder as the top-off to the horror-show epau-

lettes. Beard, bald head, bib overalls the dull, slathered
gray, the milky lusts of some mineral deficiency, Doc
says; no doubt a freshly sliced chunk or two from Mr.
Leon's alluvial walls in Mr. Leon's pocket for a sit-
down, sidewalk snack somewhere, maybe even in front
of your house if you are a schoolboy and live in our
town. Your father might look through the front blinds
and then look at you and say, Why is Mr. Leon in front
of our house tonight, and you will say, I don't know,
even though you are one of the schoolboys who pelts
Mr. Leon with anything you might want to see him stop
and bend over to pick up and lick. Rotten produce will
do, from behind the Belo Market, where you and your
friends can sometimes find Mr. Leon in summer,
perched on the broken crates and boxes of spoilage,
Mr. Leon eating stick after stick of butter that has
soured while you and your schoolboy friends scuff your
bicycles closer and closer, taunting him for a curse,
maybe even working up a spit to blow into whatever it
is he is eating carefully cradled in his clay-caked fingers. But Mr. Leon even does better than curse you.
He tells you something, something like Pussy crackles
when it's hot, you little bastards. And then he leaps
down with his canebrake stick so that you pedal off.

Flee, you little shits.

If you are a schoolboy, you go home and work out in
your mind for days what he said. Crackling. And you,
you little schoolboy, cannot hear the bacon cooking in

141

your mother's skillet the same way ever again without suffering a secret thrill.

Mr. Leon poles himself along the cart path towards us, his backwards-facing yellow tie swinging out from under one side of his domestic catskin vest to slip beneath the other, a pendulum marking time according to Mr. Leon's own personal schedule of intent, until he sits, winded, on the tombstone of Mrs. Cannady. The police had come to the caves looking for her the day she disappeared. Mr. Leon! they hollered up from the search party along the tracks. Mr. Leon! Have you seen Mrs. Cannady? And if you had been a schoolboy with them, then you would have heard nothing until someone decided to start the climb up the cliff to the caves, and then you would have heard from deep in one of the gray, hollowed throats, sounding out, Drag the lake, you bastards! and you would have seen the men from the fire department fetch the rigging and the police would have shooed you home to supper so you would have cut through the woods around back and climbed the hunting stands high in the trees over the mill pond where from up there, even in the deepening evening green of the pine forest and the algae dark around the water, you would have been the first to see the cold and green lovely glow of the alabaster body come rising to the surface on its hook, shoes and a note on the shore.

. . . . . .

The out-of-town party is showing its restive eagerness now. Hems are kneecapped, furs reshouldered, fingers tap silk shirtsleeves that are timepieced beneath. Mr. Leon pries himself off Mrs. Cannady with his stick and tick-tocks towards us. He proceeds with his stick out-struck now and it wands back and forth like a water rod. Mr. Leon's shadow seeps upon us until he is so close that the air is cool with the smell of wet clay. He stands before us, an eruption from the ground nearby, snot bulbs mud on the tip of his nose and his eyelids are so heavily crusted with clay that it is difficult to see where Mr. Leon's eyes are resting until you are sure they are resting on the mound of fresh fill from the grave. Mud forms in the corners of his mouth. The sharp teeth in the cat heads on his shoulders have been bleached somewhat since his last appearance and the flesh has drawn drier back to lend the animals a fierce-ness in death they did not possess in life. A woman in the front row from out-of-town fans herself with one hand and has the other buried in the jacket pocket of the man beside her. There are many mansions in the house of the Lord, says the man in black with the book. Mr. Leon raises his canebrake stick for silence and climbs atop the mound of fresh grave fill.

He settles into a crouch upon the mound, shrouded with his catskin vest, his anointing fist in the air. Sev-eral people stand and step back. Air begins to blow through Mr. Leon's narrowing lips, and he blows a fine mist of clayed spittle across the casket's pall. Mr. Leon draws another breath, and at once we hear the cooing of the mourning dove, a gentle fluttering touch of tongue that tapers into the chip of the lark cheated by spring. There is the whistling search for the sparrow's mate, the swallow in its field of straw, and the unanswered call of the bobwhite, unanswered, and unanswered again, then the spiraling screech of the seagull and the mimic of the mockingbird taunting us, a screen-door squeak, the cry of a cat—and then the caw of the crow, admonition, the call to fresh carrion, the feathering squawk of flight.

Mr. Leon flaps his arms, throwing mud and dust, still blowing the spittle from his foaming mouth, the worn vinyl sound of surf. Then he settles quietly into himself, hunkered on the mound of fill, a little last cooing, his eyes that are blind to us looking out at us all.

Thank you, you bastards, Mr. Leon says as he reaches down and eats from the lip of the grave.

A NOTE ON THE TYPE

This book was set in a digitized version of Bodoni Book, named after its designer, Giambattista Bodoni (1740–1813), a celebrated Italian scholar and printer. Bodoni planned his type especially for use on the more smoothly finished papers that came into vogue late in the eighteenth century and drew his letters with a mechanical regularity that is readily apparent in comparison with the less formal old style. Other characteristics that will be noted are the square serifs without fillet and the marked contrast between the light and heavy strokes.

COMPOSED BY MARYLAND COMPOSITION COMPANY, INC., GLEN BURNIE, MARYLAND

PRINTED AND BOUND BY

R. R. DONNELLEY & SONS, HARRISONBURG, VIRGINIA

DESIGNED BY HARRY FORD